TIMACK

CREATIONS

ABBOT'S KEEP

Dear Reader,

As this is the first time we have met, I will introduce myself formally.

I am Benedict Ashforth and I hope this will be the start of a unique and enduring relationship. You are now in possession of my first offering – Abbot's Keep – and I thank you for taking the time to read it.

Ghost stories are in my blood.

For as long as I can remember I have been fascinated by the possibility that ghosts are real. Surely, at times, we all sense that something is wrong or that we are not alone. But what if we are right? What if we are not alone? What if they have always been here, waiting, watching? And what if they could do much more than simply wait, and watch?

They say the dead cannot harm the living, but how can they be certain? How can we be sure?

Come now and let me guide you into the darkness, into the woods, all the way to Abbot's Keep.

Benedict Ashforth

ABBOT'S KEEP

ABBOT'S KEEP

A Ghost Story

This is for Peanut and Scampi,
the real treasures in my life.

ABBOT'S KEEP

INTRODUCTION

ABBOT'S KEEP

Creswell Manor
Oswaldkirk
Yorkshire

2nd December 1980

Dearest Annabelle,

By now you will have returned from dropping Harry
at school and I will be gone. I have been dishonest
and I apologise for all that will follow but please
know I love you, and that I will be home in just a few
short days.

Yesterday, when you asked me what the
postman had brought, I told you there was nothing,
but there was something: a letter from Simon – or
rather an account of events that have taken place
over the past month or so. I hope that once you have
read it you will understand why I have taken leave so
suddenly. You will see from the envelope that Simon
had not realised we had moved and that the letter
has taken some time in redirection to find us. If I am
to have any chance then I must go immediately.
Please understand.

I know that we have barely spoken of Simon
in recent years and you have not seen it fit to have
him around little Harry – and I have agreed – but on
reading his letter I see he is most unwell of mind and
that something terrible may have happened in
Berkshire.

I have no doubt you will wish to contact the

authorities but I beg you to refrain until I have contacted you again, which I will, just as soon as I know the truth. I must see for myself, Annabelle, must see Abbot's Keep and know if there is any truth in what he has written. Even though we are estranged he is still my brother, my only sibling, and it is what Mother and Father would have wanted.

The letter makes mention of Alexander Everett–Heath and I know at least that he does exist. He was Simon's school friend at Crowsforth some twenty years ago and in the same House as I was, although two years below, just as the letter says. I am also aware from my contacts in the city that Everett–Heath was an oil trader at one time, and does have connections with Switzerland, and also that he recently purchased a house in Berkshire – near Pangbourne – which I now take to be Abbot's Keep. Also, Natalie is spoken of, and we both know her to be real.

As for the rest, I only pray there is no truth in it. Much of what is written is clearly the imaginings of an ill mind and can have no genuine basis in reality, regardless of how authentic it all must have seemed to Simon. I am not a superstitious man and deal only in fact, as you know, and so these things are easily disregarded although I will admit that last night I was plagued by the most ghastly nightmares. In all of them Simon was there and wore the same forlorn expression. He mouthed words to me, as though desperately trying to tell me something, but no sound came. I tried also to speak, to call to him, but found that I could not. Then he simply walked away from me, into the darkness.

It is worthy of mockery but I have not been able to rid myself of his haunted face, mouthing silent words, ever since I woke this morning. I cannot ignore the sense that he may be in some dreadful danger. Yes, the mind can play terrible tricks but it is the other, more potentially factual points in his account which give rise to the gravest concern.

Please do not be too angry with me Annabelle, for not discussing matters before I left, but I know you would have tried to dissuade me from going, and also that I may have succumbed. There have been many problems with Simon over the years, and no doubt your patience has worn thin, but I must try to find him.

I have attempted to reach Abbot's Keep by phone but without success. Alexander Everett–Heath is not listed, and nor is Abbot's Keep, which in itself is quite normal. I contacted the Old Crowsforthian Society and spoke with the secretary who has no contact number for Everett–Heath. They have not heard from him since he left and only know that he attended Cambridge where he graduated with a 1st in Classics from Magdalen.

I have booked a room for the next two nights at The Weary Friar – a small inn on the Thames, just north of Pangbourne. I will contact you as soon as I have discovered what has taken place, if indeed anything has. I have left more than enough money in the usual place and have contacted the office to let them know that I will not be in over the next few days, due to 'unavoidable family issues'. Wilfred has agreed to take on my cases in my absence, else distribute the work amongst the other partners, and so please do not be concerned on this front. All is in hand.

Give Harry a kiss from me and tell him that we will finish *A Tale of Two Cities* upon on my return.

As always, all of my love to you, dearest Annabelle. I will be in touch.

Clifford

Creswell Manor
Oswaldkirk
Yorkshire

2nd December 1980

Clifford,

The weather is filthy and it will be a long and tedious drive, even in the Jaguar. It will be dark when you arrive and I hope you do not venture to Abbot's Keep at such a time. I telephoned ahead to The Weary Friar and upgraded your room to one that has views across the Thames. If you are to stay in rooms above an inn, at the very least you should be able to enjoy the surroundings – whatever the occasion – and on a barrister's salary, I feel sure our budget can stretch to this small luxury. I hope this letter reaches you first thing and that you have rested well.

Shortly after I rang, the gale picked up and bought down the telephone lines in Oswaldkirk. Since then it has been forbidding outside. No one in the village is able to call out now. The fences around the orchard are virtually destroyed and no doubt Harry will think it is brilliant.

You are right, of course. I would have tried to stop you. But you would never have 'succumbed', as you put it. When was the last time that the great Clifford Fox QC ever 'succumbed' to another's reason?

I have now had chance to read Simon's letter

and I plead with you to come home immediately, although I know you will not. Once you are decided, you are decided. It is always the same. But even though I am hurt and angry that you chose not to discuss it all with me, I cannot criticise your intentions. You are a good man, Clifford, and only have your brother's interests at heart, but it is different this time. Simon has been the greatest burden and strain on our relationship, and family at times, and now more than ever I feel that he must be left, whatever the circumstances, to find his own way. That said, I share your concerns and pray also that what is outlined in his account cannot be. It would change everything.

I will not contact the police until I have heard from you, although I consider this foolish given the nature of your work. I also agree that Simon is clearly suffering with a sickness of mind and that much of what he has recounted is simply not possible, although having read it all, especially now that the house is quiet and empty of life, I find myself looking over my shoulder and feeling that I am not altogether alone at Creswell Manor. But this is nothing in comparison with the other sensation that I have. I am not prone to superstitions either, Clifford, but I sometimes have feelings.

Paris, all those years ago, you remember. We flew from London in January, out of season. We had wanted to be in the city without the crowds. We arrived early and found accommodation in the ancient quarter of Le Marais. The hotel room looked over cobbled streets and then, across the way, to the school of ballet. We watched the girls leap and pirouette gracefully until the fog came down and obscured the view.

We went out before nightfall. You had a map of Le Marais and wanted to find L'Eglise de St Mathieu, the church you believed held clues to your ancestry. But the street names did not match those on your map and we became lost in the cobbled alleyways and deserted squares, where statues looked on at us and passersby were no more than ghostly outlines in the fog. We knew we were near the river though. The odour of the Seine was pungent in the air, lingering in every doorway and street that we found. I remember you saying as our footsteps clicked and echoed on the cobbles that we could be walking through Medieval times now; that nothing had changed here for centuries. We passed a bearded tramp on the street but did not stop to give him change.

Then, the singing. The women's voices – clear and perfect – permeating the silence. We followed the sound to the stony entrance of L'Eglise de St Mathieu. It was as though we had been led there. Inside, we sat on wooden pews in the naive and watched the nuns chanting – so faultless and beautiful that it did not seem real.

You saw I was weeping and took my hand. You assumed their voices, echoing into the silence, had overwhelmed me or maybe that, as we had found the church of your ancestors, I had been touched in some way, but you were wrong. It was something else, something non-descript, without detail, just like the Parisian facades through the fog, a steadily emerging knowledge that something terrible waited for us in Paris. When you received the urgent phone call at the hotel an hour later, with news of your mother's death, it was as though my fears had been realised, my suspicions confirmed.

I have never shared this with you, but you know that I would not fabricate stories around matters so close to your heart. I tell you this now because I have the same feeling, Clifford. It is deep within me, as distinctive as the scent of the Seine that night. Something is wrong and you must come home. It is here you belong, not at Abbot's Keep. Everything appears tangled and confused in this moment but I fear that once the fog lifts and everything becomes clear, then it will be too late.

I tried to contact Natalie earlier today but could get no answer.

There is more. Last night I too had the dreams, even though I had not yet read the story; the same dreams as yours. I saw Simon mouthing those silent words and saw the fear and sorrow stretched across his face. But more than that, you were in the dreams too Clifford and you wore the same hopeless expression and could not speak. It is not just Simon's safety that worries me. Please come home and let the police deal with this situation, if indeed there is a situation to be dealt with. Simon could be anywhere by now and I believe that you will need help to locate him. And even if you do, you cannot offer the professional help he so clearly needs. It is the same as it has been before, Clifford. He needs proper care, experienced intervention.

There is something else that bothers me about Simon's account although I do not know what it is, a small detail that I know is there but cannot see. Something about the boy, I think, but I really cannot be sure.

Please keep trying the phone this evening so we can at least talk. I love you too much to let anything happen. Harry needs you too. He will be disappointed not to see you tonight.

As ever, my love belongs to you.

Please be careful.

Annabelle

The Weary Friar
Pangbourne
Berkshire

3rd December 1980

Dearest Annabelle

Your letter arrived shortly after an excellent cooked breakfast here at The Weary Friar. Despite the unsettling content it was a bolster to receive communication from home. Thanks to you I have excellent views across the Thames and the weather has cleared this morning, leaving a thin mist over the water. As swans cut downstream the mist clears a path for them and then folds upon itself again, as though it knows instinctively of their presence and bows before them. It is something of a spectacle even from this limited vantage point, and so cheering after another fitful night.

I tried to ring last night and again this morning but without success. I will try again later and we will talk properly.

You were right that the drive was hellish. I arrived shortly after six. It was already dark and I decided not to find Abbot's Keep until morning, which will please you. I will set off shortly though, when I have finished this letter.

After finding my room last night, I washed and ventured down to the public area where I found an armchair beside the fire. It is lovely here, all twisted beams and low hanging ceilings that bulge in odd places. The furniture is deep red velvet and worn rugs cover the flagstones about the hearth. Bronze plates and hunting horns adorn the uneven walls and the place smells of old beer and cigar smoke and then, beneath that, of sweet pine-wood fires that have burnt through the years.

As I approached the bar to order a drink, I noticed an alcove in the brickwork, giving cover to a small effigy of a hooded monk, carved in black wood, crooked and holding a stick: The Weary Friar.

The Landlord, a thick-set man of around sixty with hands the size of bear paws and a mop of black and silver hair, smiled a little as he fixed his steely blue eyes on mine. For a moment, as he pulled a frothing pint from the tap, I had the thought he was ex-military or similar. He walked with a limp and rubbed at the base of his back as though nurturing an old ailment.

As he placed the beer down, I asked if he knew of Abbot's Keep.

He nodded and pointed to the wall behind the bar as though a window were there, explaining that it was less than a five minute drive. I was to follow the road adjacent to the river before taking a left towards the woodland on the hill. From there I would pass the ruined monastery in the trees and find Abbot's Keep to the right, after a junction in the road.

'Easy to miss the driveway,' he said. 'It's dark up there because of the trees and it's only a small opening.'

'Do you know the owner?'

'Mr Everett–Heath?' he said with a knowing smile. 'Comes in with his dog sometimes and sits by the fire with the papers. Likes brandy; the expensive ones. Can't say I really know him though. Friend of yours?'

I nodded and sipped my beer. 'When was the last time he came in?'

'Oh, long time, three weeks or so. Travels abroad a lot though, doesn't he?'

'Yes,' I said. 'That must be it.'

I took my pint and went to sit down again. I watched the flames lick and curl about the blackened stone and could not help but think of Simon. Where is he? What has he done? Oh, Annabelle. Please let it not be.

A few of the younger men broke into laughter at the bar. One of them took a swig of beer and said, 'Maybe he's found it and gone and bought a house in Monaco.'

My heart sank then because I knew what he was referring to. It made Simon's account all the more valid and was the very last thing that I had wanted to hear.

I finished my drink quickly and made to take an early night. I would have stayed longer but the ale is not of the same quality as at home, even though it bears the same label. But this is not Yorkshire. There are some things I do not miss from the southern counties and warm beer without taste is certainly amongst them.

I slept badly again. More than once I woke

suddenly in the stillness of my room with only the distant gushing of water passing through the weir outside to break the silence. My dreams were dark and convoluted, a nonsensical series of disquieting sights and voices which I will not trouble you with.

At one point I woke, or at least thought I had woken, to find myself in impossible darkness. I could smell something ancient and musty, like crumbling old stone. There was no sound. I reached around to find my bearings. My hands felt across rough bricks, clumpy patches of uneven cement work, wet with mould. I sensed something in the darkness with me, very close, and woke suddenly. It took me a moment to realise that I was stood bolt upright, facing the wall beside my bed. I had been feeling over the walls in my sleep. In all of my forty-six years, I have never sleepwalked.

But dawn eventually broke and with it a renewed sense of clarity and focus of mind.

My profession dictates I be rational and objective. Whatever is unearthed by all of this I will apply common sense and logic, and deal only with fact. I will find Simon and when I have, I will secure him the help you so rightly state he needs.

I understand your concerns but all will be well. There can be little doubt that I will be back in Oswaldkirk tomorrow evening and all this will be behind us. It was interesting to hear your recollections of our ill-fated trip to Paris too, and of your 'feelings'. But I put it to you that, after a long journey, you were tired and that perhaps your 'feelings' were borne of this, rather than of any paranormal perception. If you remember, the plane had been delayed and by the time we arrived we had been travelling for hours. Exhaustion, coupled with the fog and the beautiful music, would be enough to make anyone feel peculiar. We must return to Paris again for happier times.

It is also remarkable how closely your dreams resembled mine. Again, I believe I can fathom this out. We are very close, Annabelle, and always have been. Even though I lied about the letter you must have, consciously or otherwise, recognized my anxiety and known that it was something to do with Simon. There is a rational explanation for everything in life. It is only our minds that twist perception and fool us into believing that which is not possible. This is never more apparent than in Simon's account.

It is odd though, I will concede, that I am left with the same feeling as you after reading Simon's words. There is something, a small detail that bothers me, but I too am completely baffled as to what it might be. It is most unlike me. My working life – my every day – deals with the detail but this time, though I know it is there, it eludes me. I will try to ring you from the village, after I have been to Abbot's Keep.

The mist has lifted from the river now and a thin grey heron stands on the opposite bank. He is completely motionless and stares directly at me with small black eyes. It is beautiful here, but I cannot wait to be gone.

I love you, Annabelle. By the time you read this we will already have spoken and you will feel more reassured, I have no doubt.

As always, all my love to you.

Clifford

SIMON'S ACCOUNT

ABBOT'S KEEP

10th November 1980

Brother

Do not follow me once you have read this. No good can come of it.

I write only to bid farewell, for we shall not meet again in this place. I am sorry for everything, truly. Forgive it all, as I forgive you. I have been a useless brother, and son, and the most terrible husband imaginable. I write this in order that there may be a record of events that led me on this path, from which I have no hope of return.

After a time, every road is the same, no more than a friendless trail leading from one desolate location to the next, further and further from Abbot's Keep and all that took place. I walk day and night, only stopping when necessity demands. It is not good to stop for any length of time. They are easily unsettled and never far ahead. Even when I find rest beneath a bridge or in a deserted barn, it is never for long. They come back to find me, always, without conscience or mercy, and force me to continue.

Tonight, I rest in a derelict bomb shelter in the centre of a field. It is cold here and a dank smell hangs about the place. Children have carved their names into the walls and their jagged writing brings strange comfort: there is still life beyond my darkness; still happiness, even though it does not belong to me. Yes, children still laugh and play somewhere, as we once did. I hope little Harry is contented and that his life is filled with the innocence and fun that children deserve. I used to think that I was cursed for my inability to procreate. Now I know it is a godsend.

There is a small opening above my head, no more than a rough rectangle carved into the cement. I see there is no cloud to warm the land. There will be a hard frost by morning but at least I have the moonlight under which to write, and a clear view of the surrounding space, which is more important than you can imagine. There is a huddle of sheep in the far corner of the field. They fell silent and wandered away as soon as they saw me, as though they knew instinctively they were not safe in my presence. But it is good enough here for a little while. If my words become broken at times, understand that I only have short intervals before they return again. If they knew what I was doing now, there would be reprisals.

Remember the last time I saw you, Clifford? How could you forget? What a mistake you must have realised it was to have invited me, your drunken excuse for a brother – the failed architect – to the ceremony in St James' Park the night you were awarded the QC. Taking the Silk. Isn't that what you lawmen call it? The highest possible accolade bestowed upon you, soiled and ruined by your own flesh and blood. In truth I do not remember what happened, only that I awoke naked and wretched in your London flat, with no idea how I had come to be there; Mother was crying in the kitchen; Father could barely set eyes on me. You had a black eye and a cut lip.

I have become so used to those terrible moments over the years, those excruciating intersections where I cannot hide from the ugly reality that my actions have created, when I am confronted with the suffering and the pain that my deeds have inflicted on those around me. Perhaps this is my comeuppance, the ultimate punishment.

No, I have no memory of that night in St James', but everyone else does, of course. And I am sorry Clifford.

For what it's worth, and even though I have laughed insanely at life and drunk copious gallons from its heady river, I have never been happy, not truly, although more than once I have had every possible ingredient to make it so. I have sucked in the love around me like a relentless vacuum and spat it out again as though it were venom.

Yes, I have sought every last vice, every imaginable lust and pleasure to satisfy the unquenchable void but in the end, of course, it is the river that has drunk the life from me. I am an empty shell, Clifford, a damaged, leaking vessel that can never be filled, and have been ever since the problems with the Stanford building. Anyway, enough of this. No good can come from digging up the past. So I will begin now, what I set out to begin.

On 17th October, I received a letter from Alexander Everett–Heath. He was in your House at Crowsforth, but two years below. A friend of mine, not yours. I wonder if you remember him. He made his wealth from oil trading in Switzerland and retired at forty–two with more money than he could ever dispose of. We have kept in touch across the years and I am glad of it. After my stint in rehabilitation, I simply had nowhere else to go. Here is his letter:

Abbot's Keep
Pangbourne
Berkshire

17th October 1980

Simon,

Don't ask how I found you. It only matters that I have and that I am here. What are old friends for anyway, if not times like these?

There is no shame in it – quite the opposite I reckon Foxey. It's the hardest thing in the world to admit there's a problem and even harder to reach out for help. Drinking is the same as any other vice, no more and no less. I have every faith you are in exactly the right place and that getting away from everyday life is exactly the tonic (excuse the pun) you need to break the pattern. And in the end, that's all it is: nothing more than a pattern that needs altering, a habit that requires limitation, a routine that needs changing, and I know that you are strong enough.

I should have seen it coming. I mean when I saw you at Henley last year with the lovely Natalie, you looked pretty washed up. There's drunk, then there's drunk; and then there's what you were. It literally took three men to drag you out of the river, old man. I guess we're not as young as we used to be Foxey.

In case you hadn't noticed I've pretty much gone to ground these past twelve months. Quite a lot has changed. I don't work anymore for one. There's only so much black gold you can push before you need to just let go.

I bought a house in Berkshire: Abbot's Keep. You'll love it, just your kind of thing I reckon. I'm less than thirty miles from you.

I have it on good authority that you'll be released back into the wild on Tuesday 31st October and I want you to come and stay. Abbot's Keep is the perfect place to get you back into the swing of things. It'll give you a chance to collect yourself before you go back home to Natalie (if you are still an item, that is).

I fly to Switzerland early Wednesday morning for a wedding so you'll have the run of the place until I return on Friday. Don't worry about a thing. There's plenty of food and you can use my clothes if you need to. I'll be here to settle you in when you arrive.

No arguments. Anyway, you'll be doing me a favour. Abbot's Keep is pretty remote and I really don't like leaving the place empty. And then there's the small matter of Chip. I really need someone to look after and feed him whilst I'm away. I would put him in kennels but he has a nervous disposition and Springer Spaniels are notoriously bad with change.

Don't worry about ringing, just arrive. I'll be here all day Tuesday.

Look forward to seeing you.

Your old pal

AEH

I remember the drive to Abbot's Keep well enough – the rain steadily becoming heavier as I left Oxford; a nervous feeling in my stomach as the road dipped and meandered into the valley near Compton; a sense that I was drifting into a future without design.

But it was the right decision. After all, what else was I to do? Return home to Natalie and try to make things right? Tell her I had changed, stopped drinking, and that everything would work? There was too much at stake and I had already caused enough damage. If there was to be any chance of rebuilding my marriage, I would need to take things slowly, recover first; and where better than Abbot's Keep, hidden in a remote quarter of Berkshire's Green Belt.

It is ironic that Oxford's Brentwell Rehabilitation Unit is only a stone's throw from the colleges of Merton and Balliol where we graduated. The Fabulous Fox Brothers: Clifford, the talented young Lawman and Simon, the promising Architect. Your course had been five years and mine only three, and as we graduated that day, I felt the gap in our ages finally closing. We were on even ground. The world was at our feet and expectations of our success rose higher than our mortarboard caps as we threw them up towards the blue skies for the photographs. So much greatness was planned for us. We were destined for triumphs and fortune. Never for this.

I drove through Lower Parley then out towards Benfield, already a long way from anywhere, occasionally passing isolated farmhouses, disused out–buildings and deserted courtyards. And then more fields. The darkening swell of countryside bore no memory of summer now. Sheep stood motionless in rain–soaked pastures and rooks struggled to hold course against the winds.

Though I did not know it then, my old life, as I have come to see it now, was dissolving away with each mile that I drew closer to Abbot's Keep; lost amongst the rise and fall of the hills, just as steadily as the glow of Oxford's warmth was swallowed by the night.

On a muddy lane outside Pangbourne I pulled over to check the hand–drawn map Alexander had sent me whilst I had been in rehabilitation. It detailed a passage through the village, beneath a railway–bridge, to trail adjacent to the Thames for two miles or so, before a sharp left turn into a wooded area and past a ruined monastery in the trees. From there it would be a mile or so to the driveway of Abbot's Keep.

Despite conditions, villagers had taken to the streets of Pangbourne for the Halloween celebrations. A coven of green–faced witches waved broomsticks and cackled as their mother's umbrella crumpled and blew across the road before me.

Further along – beneath a railway bridge – the headlights picked out a tall man dressed in a monk's habit and a young hooded boy at his heel. Their shadows stretched impossibly around the tunnel and, as I passed, they turned away from me, but not before I caught a momentary glance at the boy's face. It was a Halloween mask, of course, but the most grotesque I had ever seen: sorrow and pain stretched across its lumpy white surface; eye sockets no more than holes of darkness; a bloody patch where there should have been an ear.

A few miles on, I found the sharp–left turn Alexander's map had indicated and ascended a single–tracked road, lined with high, unkempt hedges. There were no cars here, no signs of life. The road snaked through the countryside, past narrow turnings to the left and right which no doubt led to isolated villages, although there were no signposts. The map illustrated a straight passage from the main road towards the woodland and so I persevered, hoping not to meet other cars at each blind bend.

Eventually the road widened and tall larches, evenly–spaced, rose on either side. Something pale in the trees caught my eye; no more than a fleeting glimpse of a large crumbling wall within the woodland. The ruins. Nearly there now.

I reached the junction, turned right and then after a hundred yards or so the driveway came into view from its shaded position amongst the trees; a sparsely gravelled passage, littered with potholes and long–dead leaves, that led to darkness.

The car rattled and jutted beneath me as woodland gave way to sloping lawns, flanked with the tortured silhouettes of cherry and almond trees.

Small rabbits sat motionless on the grass, their eyes glowing points of fire in the headlights.

Then it rose up before me. Abbot's Keep.

Abbot's Keep was constructed in the classic Wealden style, its bulging exterior giving proof to the wattle–and–daub structure beneath. Ancient timbers criss–cross its white surface like dark veins and there is no doubt the wood is original. It is too thin and roughly carved to possibly have been machine–made. The windows are genuine too, jutting from the overhanging jetty on the second floor, warped and thick, each diamond–shaped pane held fast with heavy lead. Though not my favourite architecture, Tudor has its place and no more so than here, amongst dark woodland and stretching lawns. The house has stood for over 400 years and will stand long after we are gone, Clifford. Unlike the Stanford building.

I parked the car and navigated the maze of puddles to the church–like front entrance. The thick oak door whined opened as I approached and Alexander stepped out to greet me with open arms and that famous grin.

'Foxey. Too long! Far too long! Come here.'

'Trick or Treat,' I said as we hugged. My voice sounded weak and feeble, even to me.

'You look absolutely knackered. Get inside, man.'

He ushered me through to the entrance hall, a large pave–stoned area with small wooden doors leading to different areas about the ground floor and from where the ceiling reached up two floors above us. The sweet smell of a wood fire permeated the air and then beneath that, the smell of stone, chalky and old. Somewhere nearby, a dog whined and scrabbled incessantly at a door.

Alexander led the way through a low doorway and down a slender corridor. I stooped to miss beams as we made our way further down, away from the front door, but soon the ceiling rose up again and the corridor opened onto a large square kitchen, flagged in the same smooth grey stone and decorated with copper pots and various liqueur bottles of differing origins.

Here, in the light of the kitchen, we looked at each other properly.

Strange with old friends, isn't it? They grow old but somehow you don't see it, you see only the person you once knew, as though no time has passed. Alexander still possessed the same curling sandy hair and wild blue eyes and, even though wrinkles had formed about his brow, his unique energy was still apparent.

When he spoke, he made exuberant gestures with his hands, fingers spread, fanning the air like a card–magician addressing an audience.

'I'd offer you a proper drink, Foxey, but that would be completely inappropriate.' He moved to the large green Aga sitting in the corner. 'I'll put the kettle on.'

I looked up at the ceiling; rafted in tar–blackened timber and studded with wedge nails in the traditional way.

'Quite a place,' I said.

'Completely excellent isn't it. Found it about six months ago, totally fell in love and bought it the following week. Just couldn't resist. Ridiculous for a single man, I admit, but I do like my luxuries, Foxey, as you well know. Besides, a place like this might just attract the right female.' He placed the kettle on the Aga top. 'I'll show you around in a while, but first there's someone I'd like you to meet.'

He led me beneath a low archway and down another sloping passage to the west wing of the house, talking as he went.

'It was built in 1512 and later used as residence for Abbot Milroy who presided over the monastery across the field until the Reformation. I mean literally, apart from the fire in 1912 which partially destroyed the eastern side, Abbot's Keep has remained completely intact for more than four centuries. Pretty impressive, eh?'

'It's a solid structure,' I said as we neared a door at the end of the passage. 'It's all about the flying wall–plate and supporting diagonal braces.'

Alexander chuckled ahead of me and lifted his palms. 'Always the architect.'

He opened the door onto a small, stone outhouse where wellington boots and ripped towels lay strewn about the floor. A Springer Spaniel, comfortable in its blanket–filled nest, sat bolt upright as we entered and began twitching and whining as we looked on at him. Judging from the wet nose and sleek coat, the dog was young. He shot his big brown eyes nervously to Alexander, then to me, then back again, trembling and twitching and whining all the while.

'I formally introduce Chip Sharif.'

I could only smile. 'Why does your dog have a surname, and why is it Sharif?'

'Well come on! I mean look at him. He looks exactly like Omar Sharif in Lawrence of Arabia, you know, that bit when they're on the camels and the camera comes in close as he stares across the miles of desert.'

'I am sorry,' I said. 'But this Springer Spaniel bears absolutely no resemblance whatsoever to Omar Sharif.'

Alexander shook his head and lifted a long finger.

'Watch.'

Once all was quiet, aside from Chip's incessant whining, Alexander began to whistle the title tune to Lawrence of Arabia.

Almost at once, Chip stopped trembling, became incredibly still, and sat up even straighter than before. He stopped whining and lifted his head slightly, proudly even, as the music continued and looked now not at us but into the distance, with calm brown eyes and slightly raised brows, as though looking across a vast expanse of land.

'See. Now tell me again that my dog does not look like Omar Sharif in Lawrence of Arabia.'

I knelt down, still laughing, and offered Chip the back of my hand which he sniffed with interest.

'Hello, Chip Sharif.' The short fur on the top of his head was as smooth as duck's down beneath my fingers. 'Although I'm sure it was Peter O'Toole in that scene and not you.'

'Good spot,' Alexander chuckled and clapped.

'Although Chip O'Toole doesn't have quite the same ring, does it?'

As I stood back up I noticed something thin and white in the corner of the room, leaning against an old dented washing machine.

'You have a metal detector?'

'Excuse me,' said Alexander. 'That is no ordinary metal detector.'

'I didn't suspect for a moment it was.'

'Midas SureFinder 2400, top of the range. It can read up to two metres beneath the surface and differentiate between gold, silver, cast iron and nickel. It has a graphite frame which makes it lightweight and a rechargeable zinc battery that will never need replacing.'

'You're looking for treasure?'

'Damn right,' he said. 'And you're going to help me find it.'

Alexander let the dog slip through his legs and trot down towards the kitchen. He was looking at me now, properly, with unblinking blue eyes, a faint smile curling on his thick red lips.

I stared at him, trying to work out whether he was joking or not.

At that moment, the kettle began screaming in the kitchen like an abandoned child.

'Come on, Foxey. Let's get that drink.'

Alexander made tea and led us to the living area, a large square room with low-hanging ceilings and a colossal brick fire place that took up most of the western wall. Chip lay on a fleece beneath the flames and stretched himself out like a big brown rabbit, eyeing us intently and twitching every so often as the fire crackled and popped into the silence.

We talked for a while as old friends do, making sense of the years that had passed and piecing together all that had gone by, but it was a jigsaw that could never tell the full picture. There were too many pieces missing, too many blanks to know what had really happened to me over the past few years. He knew about the Stanford building, of course. We had discussed that in Henley the year before, but he knew nothing of your QC and the events that had led us to become estranged.

Estranged. Funny word isn't it, Clifford? It means nothing really, only that we have become strangers for a time. But that is the wrong word, for I know now that it will be forever. We are not *estranged*, we are lost.

I told Alexander everything that had happened since Henley; how Natalie had thrown me out of our North Moreton house; how I had wandered the streets of Oxford for two months, sleeping in my car each night before finally turning myself into the Brentwell Rehabilitation Unit.

Yes, Clifford. Two months.

Every drunk reaches the bottom eventually. The dark corner. A place where there is nowhere left to run. The place where the blade has cut too deep and only one choice now remains: do nothing and slowly bleed to death, or crawl feebly towards the light. I found my dark corner during those two months.

I existed as a vagrant, trudging aimlessly through Oxford's soaking meadows and wind-torn allotments as though I might find, in those loneliest of places, that indescribable something that would make me whole again. I found nothing of course – and so I took to drinking gin with the other degenerates and outcasts, supping from their diseased bottles in shadowy graveyards; huddled beneath ancient yews or on rotten benches; hidden from life, hidden from everything. I entertained their toothless smiles and smelt the alcohol like sweet roses and pineapple on their every breath, all the while knowing I was nothing like them really, that I belonged to a different world, that I was Simon Fox, the architect, and that I was simply just passing through. Sometimes though, at night, I would hear the bells of the city ringing out, echoing through the darkened streets, calling me, reminding me that this was Oxford, the place I had once studied so many years before. It did not seem possible.

The neo-gothic architecture that had once inspired my young mind was now no more than a stony, merciless backdrop for everything that I had never wanted to become.

Hours, days, even weeks passed with no points of reference. I was descending, free-falling into the abyss, but willingly, with intent. Drowning in self-pity, I welcomed it all. The perfect melancholy. The ultimate self-destruction. I clenched the reigns without control, drunken and screaming, and yet still wanting more.

The morning I reached my dark corner, I came around to see the young face of an undergraduate leaning over me.

'Hey, are you okay? Say something.'

Sunlight blinded me as I lay sprawled across the paves. I looked around in bewilderment, as I have done so many times before. How did I come to be here? How has this happened again? Beyond the silhouette of the young student the beautiful Venetian structure of The Bridge of Sighs arched across Catte Street. Pigeons fluttered across my line of vision as I wrestled myself into a sitting position and felt across the tangled mess of blood and hair that was my beard.

'Don't try and get up. You've hurt your head.'

I looked at him – so young; gowned, with mortar board; brown eyes sparkling in the sunshine with an abundance of life and potential so bright and overwhelming that my breath caught in my throat. So much like myself, as I had been, all those years ago.

'Stay still. Help is coming.'

Then, a terrible flash. I saw myself as that young student must have seen me, unkempt, pathetic, bloodied and dependent as I lay on the street, near death. I had been wrong, Clifford, so wrong. Yes, I was from a different world. Yes, I had been an architect, and an Oxford graduate, but now I was as hopeless and lost as all the other outcasts who I had fooled myself were of lower social standing than I. But more than that, the streets were now my keeper and my nemesis, my home and my drug. I wasn't just passing through anymore but was here to stay. Somewhere along the way, Simon Fox had disappeared, leaving only this empty shell behind. What had I done?

My weeks of trembling convalescence in the John Radcliffe Infirmary were amongst the darkest I have known. I realised then, as I lay in sterile bandaging with twenty-eight stitches to the back of my shaven head, exactly what had happened; exactly what I had lost. The problems with the Stanford building had not only destroyed my career but so many other things too. I had lost all confidence and direction. Burdened with resentment and anger, I had sought to destroy myself. I drank to forget, to ignore, to escape and to systematically bury the reality of my making. Once sober, the reality would return and so I would drink again to quieten its ugly, unwanted face.

On and on it went until now, here in this cold hospital wing with broken head, broken marriage and broken life, I had nothing left to destroy. Natalie had supported me as far as was humanly possible but had ultimately been unable to alter my determined course. Nobody could have. Once she had gone, I had crumpled completely, like an old building whose central supports had turned to rot and finally buckled under the weight. I knew then that all I wanted was to crawl back, however feebly, towards the light and make good all that I had wronged. I knew that the

Brentwell Unit would be difficult. But difficult is better than dead, and once I had recovered I could begin rebuilding my life. A second chance.

'You're going to try and win her back then, Foxey?'

'I still love her.'

We sat in silence for a moment. The fire had burnt down to a crackle of glowing embers and Chip lay fast asleep on the rug, snoring quietly and twitching his back legs every so often.

'I'm sorry,' I said. 'I've been going on.'

'Listen, you need to talk. I'm here. That's all there is, old man. Simple. You need to let it out. Totally normal.'

I had been talking for a long time and Alexander had listened without interruption. Now, I had a question for him.

'How did you find out I was at Brentwell?'

'You had to ask that, didn't you?' He grinned and fanned long fingers through the air.

'Well, it's completely embarrassing really. Totally unprofessional, and unethical. Look, the truth is I have an old friend in Oxford, Charlie Grant. I used to trade with him in Switzerland. Anyway, by chance his wife works on the clerical team at the Brentwell Unit. When she saw your file, well, she made the Crowsforth connection and asked old Charlie to find out if I knew you. Patient confidentiality completely out the window of course but at least I found you, old man. That's the important thing. A chance of fate I suppose. You were destined to come to Abbot's Keep and I'm glad of it. Now, listen, I'll be gone when you wake in the morning so I need to show you where things are before we turn in . . . Foxey, are you alright?'

Whilst Alexander had droned on, my attention had been drawn to a small hollow in the brickwork behind his armchair. Inside the cove sat a bottle of brandy with a gold chain about its neck. A small spot light had been positioned nearby to pick out the amber and golden hues of its beautiful, nectar–like contents. I swallowed the saliva that had accumulated in my mouth, feeling cold sweat build on my brow. It had been almost a month since I had tasted a drop of alcohol and now, staring at this one solitary bottle of brandy, nothing else in the world mattered. I could have easily launched across the room and smashed Alexander into hell, grabbing the bottle and glugging it down in one, never ending stream.

'Don't even think about it.' The tone in his voice snapped me back into reality, back to the fireplace, to Chip, and to Abbot's Keep. My new start.

'Especially not that one. It's Colivettia, Foxey. Italian; expensive and nearly as old as the house. Absolutely not for consumption.'

He made to get up.

'What about the treasure?' I said, hoping a change of subject would deter my cravings.

'Everything you need to know is right here.'

He lifted two leather–bound volumes from the bookcase beside him and passed them to me. The books had been earmarked in various places with neat little white markers. I took the books and scanned the gold lettering along their worn spines: *A History of Berkshire* and *Pangbourne in the Shadow of the Reformation.*

'Start with the passages I've marked out. You'll soon get the gist. I'm telling you, old man, there's gold out there somewhere. You'll make us rich if you find it.'

'You're already rich.'

'*Rich* is unobtainable. An illusion. Nothing more than a word used to describe people who look like they have cash. You never actually get *rich* because nothing's ever enough.'

I could only laugh at him.

'Alexander, you are forty-two years old and retired. You are rich.'

'You'll need this too.' He passed me a grey ring binder with a few A4 sheets clipped inside. 'It'll give you an idea of how far I've got. But save it all.' He raised a firm hand. 'Wait until tomorrow, Foxey. It'll give you something to do with Chip over the next few days. The field is at the end of the garden and runs all the way to the woodland at the southern side. I own it all, so dig at will. I've left the instruction manual for the Midas on the washing machine in the outhouse where Chip sleeps. Now, come on, get your bags and I'll escort you to your quarters. I'll show you everything you'll need on the way.'

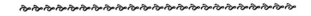

I heard a sound a moment ago. The faint rustling of

leaves beyond the cold cement walls of the bunker. Outside, the moon is high and I see the sheep have moved to a different part of the field, away from the trees. They huddle more closely than before. Safety in numbers, I suppose. A different atmosphere is settling now. I know it well.

They always bring the silence with them. They are close and I will have to stop soon.

Once Alexander had revealed the location of basic essentials, including Chip's food and dog biscuits, he led me to the second floor. As he did so I noticed an arched doorway set into the wall beneath the stairs. The oak door was decorated in heavy medieval hinge-work and looked thick as a tree.

'The cellar,' Alexander said, as he creaked his way up the staircase. 'Out of bounds. It's full of old wine Foxey and I don't reckon you could control yourself.'

'Thanks for the vote of confidence.'

Alexander gave me a bedroom on the eastern wing, at the end of a slanting corridor furnished with small brass bell-lamps. The room was cold but neatly arranged: a small four-poster bed, burgundy carpets and leaded windows looking out into blackness.

'I need to be at the airport by four a.m. so I'll not wake you when I leave. Take care old man and it's great to have you here.'

It took me a while to sleep. I heard Alexander creep back down stairs and cork the bottle of wine he had obviously been craving all evening. I wanted to get up and join him for one but I knew it would never end if I did. One was never enough and nor was twenty.

I woke in the early hours to the ticking and groaning of radiators about the house. Shortly afterwards, I heard Alexander get up and do his level best to leave the house without waking me. His Porsche roared to life outside and began rattling down the driveway. Soon he was out of earshot and I was left in the silence again. The clouds had cleared now and a stream of moonlight found its way through a gap in the velvet curtains, reflecting small droplets of rain on the crooked ceiling above my bed.

It was then I felt it for the first time; something intangible just beneath the brooding silence of the house, as though someone were waiting patiently, absolutely still, deep within the darkness of Abbot's Keep. It was a strange feeling but I could not deny it was there and every bit a real as Chip's frightened whining far below in the kitchen. And there was something else too.

I hadn't felt this way since Crowsforth, when Mother and Father had left me, at age 10, in North Yorkshire in those unfamiliar surroundings.

Yes, you were there too Clifford but, late at night when all the other boys in the dormitory were sleeping, being so far from home and anything I had ever known, it was a lonely place to be. Lonely like this, like Abbot's Keep. It clung in the air around me like an invisible veil, a terrible sense of longing and sadness that I wasn't sure was of my own making, or was being impressed upon me.

ᕒᕒᕒᕒᕒᕒᕒᕒᕒᕒᕒᕒᕒᕒᕒᕒᕒᕒᕒᕒᕒᕒ

I see them now, across the field, in the shadows. At first I thought it was deer moving in and out of the trees, their pale boughs bright in silver moonlight.

But the silence is here properly now, and I must follow, before I am made to follow. It is better that way.

Creswell Manor
Oswaldkirk
Yorkshire

4th December 1980

Clifford,

Where the hell are you?

I am at the end of my tether here. I am so angry and worried, you have no idea. You have not telephoned as you said you would, even though the phone lines are working. I have rung The Weary Friar numerous times over the last twelve hours. They tell me you did not return last night, although your belongings are still in your room.

I have gone against your wishes but without regret. I had no option but to contact the police. It is now eleven am and there is still no sign of you. I have told them everything, and passed over Simon's letter. They are on their way to Abbot's Keep.

You were a fool to have gone to Berkshire alone. I would drive down myself to find you but it is not right that Harry should suffer any anxiety during the school week.

I said before that I could not criticise your intentions, that you are a good man and only have your brother's interests at heart, but the more I think about it the more I understand. It is not just your brother's interests you have considered, but yours too.

Yes, Clifford, there is a part of you that yearns for reconciliation. You were terrified, weren't you, that it would never come about if you did not find him. But what happened with the Stanford building is ancient history. You cannot change the past. It is done.

I have prayed and prayed for your safety. When you return I will never let you out of my sight.

Come home. We love you.

Annabelle

The history of the monastery at Pangbourne is an interesting one, Clifford.

By lunchtime the following day, sat beside the fireplace in the quietness of Abbot's Keep with Chip resting silently at my feet, I had read through all the passages that Alexander had marked out. Every now and then I would get up and make a cup of tea or add logs to the fire to warm the living area.

I placed a large Atlas of Britain in the alcove where the Colivettia sat so that it was hidden from view as I read. By the time I had finished the sun was beaming through the windows and across my face, beckoning me outside.

Listen:

In March 1531, a Benedictine monk named Fr Angus Milroy was expelled from the monastic community at Pentineux in North Yorkshire, for attempting to steal apostolic relics from the Abbey. It is documented that, whilst the other brethren prayed at Mass during Lent, he descended to the crypt where he prised opened the glass case that housed a rib bone thought to have belonged to St Mathew.

Now an outcast from the Benedictine order, Milroy headed across the Channel to Europe from the docks at Grimsby and travelled south on foot through France, stopping at churches in Chermone and Florac under the pretence that he remained a member of the monastic community and needed rest for the night.

Records from the chapel of Sheltroix le Marie, in Lonjagnes, Gorge du Tarn, describe a tall monk dressed in black robes, weary from travelling, arriving for a night's rest. In the morning there was no sign of the monk.

The chapel's relics were missing, along with the sacramental chalice and plate used for the Eucharist. Another account from Pau, on the Spanish border, describes again a tall thin monk with piercing black eyes stealing gold from the monastery at St Therese d'Ispagniac.

In November of the same year, Milroy returned north to Paris where he found monasteries and churches willing to pay gold pieces for the stolen artefacts. Having found a way to turn his haberdashery into solid gold, he exploited it without conscience. During this period, he befriended a homeless peasant child from Northern France by the name of Antonio Goupil. Antonio's role was clear: to help smuggle the gold from Northern France back to English shores. So began their burdened journey to the north coast of France where, just south of Calais, Milroy secured the services of a fishing vessel that would aid their passage across the Channel.

The night before they set sail, whilst taking rest in the fishing village of Verdane, Milroy allegedly came upon the young Antonio Goupil stealing gold coins from the casket that they had carted some two hundred miles.

In true Medieval style, the punishment was brutal and without mercy.

Milroy cut off the boy's ears and severed his tongue with a farrier's hoof parer, and then gelded him.

Milroy, undeterred in his purpose for the child, forced him to continue through the night, mutilated and bleeding, to Dover, to seek new lodgings with his ill-found gains. With Goupil hauling the gold behind in the wooden cart, he headed across the southern counties in search of a suitable residence, eventually finding a disused farm in Pangbourne.

The land consisted of a farmhouse, twenty-four acres of land and a gatehouse, later named Abbot's Keep.

The abandoned farmhouse was swiftly converted into boardings. A monastery was created and a new monastic order formed: Geltrentine, a unique denomination with Abbot Milroy as its founder. A few of the villagers were converted and reaped the land to create self-sufficiency for the brethren. Abbot Milroy took lodgings at the gate house, Abbot's Keep, where he kept Antonio Goupil as his servant, whilst he presided over the monastery at the end of the field.

For a time the community existed in peace and prayer, albeit under the controlling eyes of Abbot Milroy. Whilst stories of his cruelty and ferocity were abundant, for the most part the monks survived in harmony, farming the fields and achieving self-sufficiency. At the western end of the farmland an orchard was planted to provide cider for future years, but it was all badly timed.

By the winter of 1535 the Reformation was well under way and the Dissolution of the smaller monasteries around England had begun.

Whilst King Henry VIII's men primarily targeted Catholic communities, Abbot Milroy's monastery, rumoured to harbour untold wealth within its stone walls, was pillaged and burnt to the ground. The Geltrentine monks were rounded up and thrown screaming to the flames. From this point, the stories conflict.

In most legends, Abbot Milroy and Goupil were found by the King's men and tortured in attempts to prise the location of the gold from them. They died in captivity, never giving clue to its whereabouts.

In other stories, the Abbot and the boy fled the fire never to be seen again, leaving the gold buried somewhere in the fields around the monastery.

I sat quietly for a long time after I had finished reading, watching flames lick and curl about the logs in the hearth as I imagined the monastery being torched to the ground. I couldn't help wondering what had become of Abbot Milroy and his disfigured assistant. Something else too, I kept thinking of the robed figure I had seen the previous night, beneath the railway bridge in Pangbourne. The child at his side who wore the terrible mask.

A chill ran through me. It occurred to me then how well-known the legends must be locally, to wear those clothes on a Halloween night, and to be recognised.

I thought of Goupil too. How could anyone hurt a child in that way?

Chip trotted into the room and wagged his tail

around my feet, breaking my chain of thought.

I opened Alexander's ring binder and found, set out neatly on graph paper inside, a hand-drawn overview of Abbot's Keep and the surrounding acreage. At the upper part of the page Abbot's Keep was a large rectangle between two larger squares, the lawns to north and south. The lawn on the southern side gave way to an open area which took up most of the page. Approximately half the area, from east to west, had been cross hatched with pencil to mark the section of the field Alexander had already covered.

At the bottom end of the page, small hand-drawn trees illustrated where woodland began and, in this area, Alexander had roughly pencilled-in broken brickwork, indicating the monastery ruins.

'OK, Chip Sharif,' I reached down and stroked him. 'Let's take a look.'

In the outhouse, I slipped on a pair of Alexander's wellington boots and headed into the sunshine.

It was the first time I had seen the exterior of Abbot's Keep properly and so out of interest I circled its perimeter to the eastern side where, according to Alexander, the building had suffered fire damage in 1912. Whilst there was no visible damage to the brickwork, lighter patches on the structure made it clear that the property had been partly destroyed and I estimated at least two metres were missing from the original construction here.

I made my way across the southern lawn to the beech hedge that marked the edge of the field beyond. There was an earthy smell in the air from the night's rainfall and in places the lawn was waterlogged and muddy. Chip trotted on ahead, occasionally stopping to sniff the sodden ground as we neared an old gate that gave view to a clumpy green expanse, sloping towards woodland.

The sun was warm on my skin and I saw that a light vapour was rising from the surface of the field; moisture returning to air. In amongst the dark trees and crows nests at the bottom of the field I could just make out the pale ruins of the monastery.

As we passed through the ramshackle iron gate, Chip began rooting in the undergrowth, darting in and out of shadows, making his way further and further around the circumference of the field, seeking out birds in brambled areas and barking as they took wing. Interesting to watch a gun dog at work, Clifford, the years of breeding and inbreeding creating the perfect hunting animal. A bit like us, with our decades of family tradition, wealthy blood and pride, all mixed up together to create successful men of us; reared to win. But there's only so much that can be controlled. In the end, life just happens, and so does death.

Once Chip had circumnavigated the entire area, he traversed the field, scouting from edge to the edge, methodically checking every inch of grass for signs of life.

๛๛๛๛๛๛๛๛๛๛๛๛๛๛๛๛๛๛๛๛๛๛

Tonight I shelter in a derelict water tower that sits like a redundant brick chimney at the summit of a grassy hill. There is a different smell in the air here; the faintest tang of salt that tells me our pathway East is nearly at an end. Earlier, under moonlight, I saw the distant shimmering of water on the horizon. The muscles in my legs burn from the long hours of walking but I do not have much time. They will return soon and there is more urgency and purpose in their method now; but I will continue writing until the silence comes.

๛๛๛๛๛๛๛๛๛๛๛๛๛๛๛๛๛๛๛๛๛๛

In the woodland at the base of the field the earth gave way easily under foot. The gentle sloping of the terrain towards this point meant that rainwater gathered here, making the ground boggy and swamp-like. Behind me, Chip sat in the field with upturned nose, refusing to follow as I made my way towards the ruins. The dark scent of long-dead leaves permeated the air and, far above, crows fluttered restlessly in their nests, occasionally snapping at twigs and cawing into the quietness.

The monastery ruins consist of a clutter of dilapidated buttresses and a stone archway rising up from the ground with no supporting walls to either side. It had once have served as the entrance to the main building but now, crumbling and ivy-covered, it stands alone amongst the trees. Beyond the archway, the remnants of the outer-walls rise up like crooked, rotting teeth in various places about an irregular rectangle some ten metres in length.

It was an odd feeling standing inside the monastery walls, as though I were treading on ground where I had no right to set foot. Even though I knew the land belonged to Alexander, I couldn't shake off the sense that I was not wanted here; that I was trespassing and being made to feel ill at ease somehow.

For a moment the crows became silent and I had the strangest feeling that someone tall was standing directly behind me, very close. Yet when I turned there was nothing, only the crumbling stone archway and the gentle creaking of the larches as they swayed in the wind.

The Midas 2400 was easy to get to grips with and every bit as impressive as Alexander had said. Three dials protruded from the small metal box three-quarter lengths up its graphite stem. The first was marked **DC** (Depth Calibration); used to select the depth beneath the ground at which the Midas would detect metal. The second was notched with various settings: **G** (Gold), **S** (Silver), **I** (Iron), **N** (Nickel) and **A** (All metals). The third was simply marked **V** (Volume).

I selected All Metals and took the detector outside to calibrate depth.

I switched the Midas on, which immediately hummed to life and began wailing varying frequencies into the silence like a mistuned radio. Beside me, Chip whined as a passing frequency became uncomfortable for his sensitive hearing.

Next, I held the detector approximately half-a-metre from the surface of the grass. This was the depth at which the detection of metal would be limited to. Using the DC control, I tuned-in the frequency until the oscillating tones became a single, monotonous hum.

I dropped my car keys to the ground and lifted the Midas around two feet from the grass before passing the detector over them. The low hum of the detector rose immediately to a single, shrill tone as it identified the metal. Done.

I spent the rest of the afternoon in the field with a shovel and an excited Chip. Alexander had driven cricket stumps into the ground at various intervals to mark out the area that had been covered already. I started at the eastern corner and made a steady path towards the trees at the south. Within minutes, the Midas identified metal beneath the surface.

I remember thinking as I began digging how great it would be if, in the first place I looked, I found a great big stash of gold. Having dug perhaps half a metre beneath the surface, the blade hit something solid and sparks flew around the hole at my feet. I reached into the mud to pull out a rusty old horseshoe. I took it as a sign of good luck and continued down the field.

Every now and then the high pitched whine would sound and Chip would come running to watch me dig another hole. I uncovered three more horseshoes and a selection of old cans and mangled nails over the next two hours. I was tired from digging but felt so alive. Oxford's grimy streets and the John Radcliffe Infirmary could not have been further from my mind and I realised, at around three o'clock, that I hadn't even thought of alcohol for the whole day. Progress felt good, and so did being in the countryside with sunshine warming my face.

As I continued, my thoughts turned to Natalie; her long dark hair and green eyes, the way her dimples came to life when she smiled. How I missed her, Clifford. It was difficult to imagine that she may never take me back. All I had was hope.

My mood blackened some time later, as I began to think of the Stanford building and all that had happened during 1978. I suddenly craved the nectar that would dissolve everything into oblivion but I had to keep strong, had to keep searching, keep carving out the wet soil until it passed again. In rehabilitation they give you ways of dealing with cravings; they tell you to keep your hands busy – Aversion Therapy. One doctor even told me to take up knitting but right now I just needed to dig, and keep digging and digging, until it was gone.

I am diagnosed with Addictive Personality Disorder, Clifford. APD, now that makes it better, doesn't it? Give it a name and it all goes away, right? Apparently, I am drawn to activities that present short term gain. Have a cigarette, feel relaxed. Take a punt on a horse, feel excited, then lose, but do it again anyway to feel the exhilaration. Have a drink, feel peaceful, so have another and another. Digging for buried treasure was the perfect therapy, a way of achieving short term satisfaction but without the damage. At least, that was the theory.

At one point, the crows in the woodland became unsettled and cawed and flapped violently in amongst the tree tops. As I looked over in the direction of the ruins, I caught a momentary glimpse of a thin shadow passing over the archway there but, as I squinted into the sunlight to make it out, it was gone.

I selected the **G** (Gold) setting because I'd had enough of unearthing nails and horseshoes.

I covered a large area with no results, all the while brooding over the Stanford building and the mess that was my life. I had long understood that I would never again be commissioned to create a new structure yet for some reason it was goading me now, as I continued scanning the land with the Midas in small sweeping motions. No, I would never again have control of a building project.

Nobody hires an architect who designs buildings that kill people.

I felt the familiar hatred brewing up in those minutes, Clifford. Hatred of you, hatred of your success, hatred of your marriage and hatred of your ability to have children. Hatred of the letters, QC, after your name.

Just then I heard someone laughing at the side of the field and I turned to see an old man dressed in a dark wax jacket, crouching down and stroking Chip. As I made my way towards him he continued laughing and looking at me from behind misty blue eyes.

'You'll never find it,' he said, standing up and resting his hand on the fence between us. 'Never in a million years.'

I slammed the shovel hard into the ground and glared at him.

'Why don't you shut your mouth, you stupid old bastard. What the fuck do you know anyway?'

Well, that did it. I watched as he hobbled away across the fields like a frightened animal.

Later, as Chip crunched through dog biscuits in the kitchen, I wondered how I must have looked to the old man; drenched in sweat; covered in earth and grime, glaring and shouting like a madman.

Looking now across the lawn and watching dark buzzards circle far above Abbot's Keep, I felt calm, and disbelief that I had become so angry.

But that's withdrawal for you, Clifford. It hurts.

Two dead people. It is never far from me; their names etched into my mind as deeply as the engravings on their tombstones: Maria Jones (36) and Josephine Elliot (22).

The problems with the Stanford building were not of my making, at least not from a design perspective. That is the truth, Clifford, although the papers would tell their own story; the one that would make easy sense to the world.

Even from the first rough sketches, it was clear that the structure would be complex and require every ounce of knowledge and skill that I had attained. Bringing a Parisian structure to the banks of the Thames did not come without unique areas of risk. All were carefully assessed and quantified. It took three years and two months to make it happen, to make it real, and to make it safe. The perfect Museum of Modern Architecture, set on the South Bank, at Stanford.

When the western supporting wall collapsed, killing the two women as they fell from the upper floor, it simply didn't make sense. No significant weight had been impressed on the area and no matter how hard I tried to calculate the possibility, it seemed unattainable. It was only later I found evidence that the cement used in a number of the supports was too porous. Thames water had sunk into a foundation on the western side which, in turn, acted like a sponge. The rest is history. It was not the design, Clifford, which led to the deaths of Maria Jones and Josephine Elliot but a failure in the engineering company's materials. The building was borne of my imagination – every calculation of my making – but I did not lay the bricks myself. I did not mix the cement.

I used to think that the women were like me, their futures having been taken, wrenched from their grasp. Now, sitting in the warmth of Abbot's Keep I realised, for the first time, I could still have a future, if only I could control myself and become strong again.

It took me a long time to forgive you, Clifford, which I have now done, even though you have never apologised to me.

Once showered and changed, I cooked beans on toast and sat by the fire with Chip. Outside the wind had picked up and howled around the structure of the house. A magnolia branch tapped at the window like an old dry finger and every now and then Chip lifted an ear and gave me a slightly concerned look before resting down on his paws again.

There was a different feeling now, in Abbot's Keep, one I had not experienced before. I was strangely comfortable, as though I had always lived here and had simply come home after being a long time away. What had Alexander said? *'You were destined to come to Abbot's Keep.'*

I took off my shoes and socks and stretched out my aching legs. The fire was roaring and crackling but still I could hear the wind outside, growing steadily in strength as it brushed and whistled across the ancient structure of Abbot's

Keep. In the alcove above the fireplace, the Colivettia sat covered by the atlas but my cravings were gone now and I could relax properly. I picked a novel from the shelf and began reading.

I awoke some hours later, certain a loud noise had sounded somewhere within the house. The logs on the fire had died down to a blackened crisp and a chilly silence hung in the air. Chip had woken also and was staring at the window above my head with a startled expression. As I turned to look I caught sight of movement beyond the glass. A dark shape passing the window outside.

I rushed to the front door and opened it. The gale, in full swing, almost forced the door back into my face.

'Who is it? Who's there?'

But there was nothing, only the wind blustering leaves across the driveway. For a moment I thought I heard someone whisper something next to me, but as I listened harder all I could hear was the wind feeling its way around the house and the distant creaking of the larches at the bottom of the field.

Chip followed me upstairs to the bedroom with tail between legs. I had tried to settle him in his basket but every time I closed the door he whined and barked and scrabbled until I returned. He did not want to be alone.

Later in bed, I listened to sheets of rain hammer against the window beside me with Chip curled at my feet like a big warm cat. Before I went to sleep I peered through the darkness into the garden. The clouds parted momentarily, casting a silvery light across the estate.

Past the end of the garden, far towards the bottom of the field, I glimpsed a tall figure rushing towards the larches near the ruins, but then a cloud drifted over the moon and the landscape fell to darkness again.

I woke in bed the following morning, bathed in warm sunshine. I had no idea then, Clifford, that this would be the day that would change everything.

※※※※※※※※※※※※※※※※※※※※※※

Tonight I have found shelter in a redundant lighthouse on a rocky cliff-top, hundreds of feet above the water. I had to break the lock to get in but it was freezing and I had no choice. After I had made my way up the spiralling iron steps to the observatory, I tried to rest for a little while but it is no use. The sound of the sea smashing against the rocks below fills me with dread, for I do not know where they will lead me next.

The small rounded space in which I sit is illuminated by the moon and the stench of the sea is strong here. Somehow crabs have made their way from the beach, all the way up the rock face and into the lighthouse. Their shells litter the damp surface around me and glisten in the light. Looking at them now, I wish I were dead too, although I don't imagine it would change anything. There is a skeleton here too. A seagull, half feathers, half bones. He must have found his way in here somehow, not realising he would never escape. In a way we are the same.

Still, at least I will be able to hear them when they return. I have shut the lighthouse door and wedged an old piece of driftwood against it. When it is opened, the wood will fall to the metal and echo through this tower.

I gave Chip his breakfast and went straight into the sunshine to survey the storm damage. Leaves and twigs lay strewn across the grass and the gate at the end of the lawn had come away from its hinges completely. At the field Chip immediately went into hunting mode and began his usual systematic check of the area as I made my way towards the ruins. A tall larch had fallen from the woodland there, its roots protruding like a huge clumpy spider from its base.

It was a big tree, forty metres at least and for some reason I was pleased it had not fallen into the ruins, but instead into the field. Even though there was no real structure to the remnants of the monastery, it would have been a shame to see what was left of the archway destroyed like that.

It was only as I made my way back up the field and finally reached the gate by the lawn, that I noticed Chip was missing.

At first I was not panicked, thinking he had chased a rabbit, followed a trail or perhaps gone exploring for a short while. I went back inside briefly to get the Midas. When I returned there was still no sign. I paced the perimeter of the field twice, checking through the undergrowth as I went. Nothing.

I walked into the woodland and around the ruins, calling as I went, but the only sound here was the occasional cawing of the crows above and the creaking of the larches. For some reason, as I stood amongst the ruins of the monastery, I knew instinctively that something was wrong.

I returned to the old gate and marched across the lawn to the back door in case Chip was waiting for me there, but it was no use. I went back inside the house and ran upstairs, checking each room and looking across the grounds from each vantage point.

Next, I hurried down the driveway to the main road where I strode in each direction for a mile or so, checking he had not been run over and left on the roadside. Afterwards, I returned to the field and searched it all again, making sure he was not caught in a trap or tangled in barbed wire within the undergrowth. I even checked beneath the fallen larch.

Later in the day, after an hour of fruitless biscuit-box rattling in the field, I drove around the surrounding areas, crawling slowly along every road and muddy pathway I could find, occasionally getting out to scan nearby fields and call out his name. Then, at around three o'clock, it began to rain heavily.

I knew at this point there was a real problem. Chip was already two hours late for lunch and would have returned home if he could have. I have never known a dog not to return for food without good cause.

How had it happened? I ran through the events over and over again: We had entered through the gate and Chip had rooted in the undergrowth around the perimeter of the field, moving clockwise. I had walked to the felled tree and, after a few minutes, had turned back again in the direction of the house. I had seen Chip at that point to my right, near the bottom of the field, where the woodland began.

But by the time I had reached the gate some five minutes later, he was gone.

It made sense that something must have happened to him in the vicinity of the woodland.

Drenched to the bone, I went to check once more, both in and out of the trees but could find no trace. The weather was worsening now and I stumbled out from the trees and sat on the felled larch to rest for a moment. The wind picked up and I stared towards the top of the trees as they swayed against the gun metal sky. Then I heard it. The sound that I had wanted to hear so badly over the past five hours. It was faint but unmistakeable: Chip's small bark and whimper somewhere close by.

'Chip!' I shouted. 'Here Boy!'

I waited long minutes in the beating rain for him to return from the woodland but when he didn't appear, I began to think I had imagined it.

There it was again. A muffled bark somewhere nearby.

I hurried in the direction of the sound, towards the centre of the field. I could hear him again, louder this time. Nothing made sense. I could hear the dog, whimpering and barking very close by, but he was nowhere to be seen. Here I stood, alone in a large acreage of grassland. Then came one last muffled bark, directly beneath my feet, and I understood.

I took off my jacket and left it on the ground to mark the spot, then sprinted back to Abbot's Keep for the shovel.

I lay flat on the soaking grass when I returned, my ear pushed to the ground until I heard him again. He sounded frightened and I patted hard against the wet ground, 'Don't worry Chip, I'm getting you out. Stay there.'

I dug in shallow rafts, ripping turf from the top soil so as not to hurt Chip, but soon realised he was a long way beneath the surface. So I buried the blade more deeply into the ground until a large square hole formed at my feet which rapidly began filling with rain water. I struck the soil again and again until I hit hard chalk.

I was certain Chip was close now. If I could just get past the chalk. I gave one final drive into the ground. As I did, the land gave way beneath me and I fell.

For a moment I did not understand. I gaped stupidly at the chalky earth around me as I lay deep within the trench that had formed. Rain stung at my face as I looked up to see how deeply into the ground I had fallen.

Chip gave a pathetic whimper and I scrambled to my knees and began clawing away at the mud to find him until my fingers stiffened with pain. Beside me, the shovel protruded vertically from the soil. As I pulled it free Chip wailed like a scolded child. My heart sank then because blood was dripping from the shiny metal surface.

I tore frantically at the soil until my fingers brushed across his sleek wet coat. It was easy then to dig around his body and bring his face to the air so that he could breathe properly. As I cradled his shivering, bloodied body in my arms and stood up, he whimpered again and stared at me with wild, pleading eyes.

I lifted him up above my head, onto the surface of the field, then clambered out of the trench.

I knelt beside him and moaned aloud at the sight of his injury. I saw now what had happened. As the ground had collapsed, the blade of the shovel had sliced through his neck, creating a deep gash that now pumped blood into the soil around us.

It was too late, Clifford. All I could do was watch the life drain from his trembling body. He looked beyond me, up into the clouds, as he lay on the cold soil. His eyes bore the same far–away Lawrence of Arabia look I had seen when I'd first met him. Then he simply stopped trembling and lay still.

He was dead and I was alone in the rain, with the distant cawing of crows in the woodland.

❧❧❧❧❧❧❧❧❧❧❧❧❧❧❧❧❧❧❧❧❧❧❧

A moment ago the driftwood clanked to the floor, sending hollow echoes up the stairwell and around the moonlit observatory. At first I thought the wind may have pushed the door open down there, but now I sense the malice in the atmosphere and know they have returned. Their whispers fill the silence.

They wait for me.

❧❧❧❧❧❧❧❧❧❧❧❧❧❧❧❧❧❧❧❧❧❧❧

Back inside, I wrapped Chip's lifeless body in his favourite towels and laid him to rest in the outhouse basket. It hadn't seemed right to leave him in the cold but I wasn't ready to bury him yet either. It was a nightmare. Alexander would be back in the morning and I had no idea how I would explain this. It had been an accident, of course, but how would that make it better?

I found a bottle of Scotch in the dining room cabinet, poured out a large glass, and gulped it down in one. I almost gagged but five minutes later, realising it was exactly what I needed, poured another.

I went upstairs to my bedroom and gazed over the field. From here I could see the felled tree, and also the muddy earth that had given way. But it was different now.

Since I had carried Chip back inside, more of the ground had subsided, the collapsed trench now running some twenty metres from the base of the fallen tree, right to the centre of the field where Chip had died. It was a deep gully and did not meander, pointing straight towards the east of the house like a dark vein.

I took a swig of whisky and ran through the events as they must have occurred: The tree had fallen, exposing an entrance which Chip had found and climbed inside. At some point, the entrance had buckled and become concealed again, explaining why Chip could not get out – and why I had been unable to find him.

Looking at the trench now, it occurred to me that the underground tunnel that Chip had found was at least a metre and a half high and definitely man-made. No animal could have created a channel this large or straight.

I smiled a little then, Clifford, as I continued to drink, because I'd had an idea and, far-fetched though it seemed, I needed to be sure.

Outside, the rain had stopped but light was fading fast, clouds now inked with purple and black. I hastened to the edge of the woodland, beside the fallen larch, where I re-set the Midas depth calibration to the approximate depth of the trench. I selected Gold and began scanning the subsided ground until I reached the centre of the field where Chip had died. Nothing.

It made sense to me that, even though the field became level here, the tunnel must continue beneath the ground towards Abbot's Keep in the same, straight direction, and was intact. I continued in a straight line, without deviation, imagining the tunnel beneath me, all the way to the house.

As I crossed the lawn, the Midas was completely silent.

Around two metres from the house, I realised that if the tunnel did exist here then it did not run under the house as I thought it might, but instead passed wide, approximately one metre from the eastern face.

Just then the Midas sounded a quiet but definite tone.

I examined the vicinity again. Yes – though

the signal was difficult to make out, almost hidden beneath the monotonous hum – every time I passed the Midas over the area a slight change in frequency was audible. If the Midas really could differentiate between metals, it was gold.

I thought about the spade in the outhouse but it was too dark to start digging now. Besides, this area formed part of the lawn and Alexander would not appreciate it. *Oh sorry, yes, Chip is dead and I've dug up your lawn too.*

I went inside and poured another whisky, pleased that I had at least located something after so much searching. I put some logs on the fire and opened Alexander's ring binder where I pencilled–in the tunnel, as I imagined it, running from the ruins, right across the field, under the lawn and just past the eastern face of Abbot's Keep. I stared at the picture for a while. It made sense that there should have been a secret passage from the monastery to Abbot's Keep, so that there could be an escape route for Abbot Milroy if the need arose.

Then it came to me. I was stupid not to have realised it before.

The tunnel *had* run directly beneath the house for centuries, just as I had originally thought, but the fire in 1912 which had partially destroyed the eastern side, meant that it no longer seemed that way. Now the tunnel appeared as though it fell just wide of the house. But did it?

I poured another whisky and pondered this for a long time as I stared into the licking flames.

Outside, darkness had fallen, the glass in the

leaded window beside me reflecting my gaunt face, which flickered in the firelight. In those minutes, a heavy silence settled over the room, oppressive and charged with anticipation, as though the house itself were reading my every thought and was clenching with malice at my intentions.

I knew then that I had to look, just to see if I was right.

I wandered down the crooked passageway towards the staircase, already feeling the whisky affecting my balance. The small bell lamps on the walls seemed dimmer than usual as I neared the cellar door, casting flitting shadows across its ancient surface. I hesitated for a moment before turning the handle as though unconsciously, through some inner sense, knew that taking this action would have unknown consequences. But it was too late for indecision.

The church–like steps leading to the cellar were from the original build, each ledge smooth and worn through centuries of use. Above me a single bulb hung from a tar–stained beam, lighting the way as I made my descent. With each step, the air grew colder. The silence here was different than the rest of the house, a strange, watchful silence, conscious and keenly aware.

At the bottom step I pulled the drawstring above by my head and the main lights flickered on.

The cellar was a larger than I had imagined, with vaulted ceilings running its entire length. The northern wall was racked from base to top with dusty wine bottles and the scent of old grape and crumbling cork permeated the air. I felt I had reached heaven as I lifted a bottle randomly and brushed the dust away to read its label.

The southern side was dedicated to miscellaneous items littered about the space: shovels, picks and rakes. On a warped wooden shelf lay a hammer with various rusty nails and bolts to its side, a torch, and a cork screw. With each clicking step I took across the flagstones, I became more aware of the oppressive silence. It was the same feeling I'd had at the ruins, a feeling of being unwanted or of being watched with intent. But I was alone here.

I corked the bottle and glugged some down before moving towards the area that I had come to inspect: The eastern wall.

I saw it immediately of course and knew that I was right. The eastern wall was constructed of modern brick and out of keeping with the rest of the cellar. I picked the torch from the shelf and shone it towards the top of the wall, and there it was: a pale brick, deeply inscribed with the numbers, 1912. I ran a hand across the wall's rough surface, then a forefinger along the cement work which crumbled like dust towards the floor. Too much sand in the cement mixture, just like the Stanford building, only this time it would not be Thames water that destroyed the structure.

The bricks were of low quality, crumbling away easily under the force of the hammer as I struck the centre of the wall again and again. Within minutes, two fell through to the other side with great rumbling thuds and the cement gave way more fluently; causing more bricks to dislodge and be effortlessly pulled away by hand. Once I had created a rough archway in the wall that enabled access to the other side, I stood and swigged at the wine, catching my breath and staring into the void that had not seen life, since 1912.

I had been right so far but knew that what lay inside would be the ultimate test.

I stepped across the threshold.

The torch beam shone into blackness, picking out swirls of dust as my footsteps unsettled all that had lain untouched for over sixty years. I noticed charring on the stone here and there, no doubt from the flames that had destroyed the area above ground. A solitary blackened crucifix, cast in iron, hung alone on the northern wall but the small rectangular space was bare of any furniture or fittings, other than an ancient wooden bookcase that sat against the southern wall. It was what lay behind the bookcase that I needed to see.

I placed the torch on the ground and scraped its wooden weight across the floor until I could see clearly all that lay behind.

Now, shining the beam, I saw immediately that a large round opening had been neatly created in the wall, and then roughly patched back over with a mess of grey stone and dried mud. It was too confused and untidy to have been enclosed from this side. There was no question about it. The cavity had been sealed from the inside. There could be no doubt either, that I had found the mouth of the tunnel.

Before I began, I went through to the main cellar area, found a suitable trowel and popped open a bottle of *1962 Chateau Latour* – fantastic, although tinged with a sharp undertone I was unaccustomed to.

The dried earth bonding the stones together came away easily under the trowel's blade, leaving only bulky rocks to cover the entrance. As I pulled the first heavy stone away to expose the darkness within, the tunnel sucked in a gasp of air, as though taking a sharp breath after centuries of suffocation. In reality though, I concluded, the earlier collapse of the tunnel had likely created a vacuum of some kind. Undeterred, I pulled more and more of the stones away to finally expose the tunnel in all its glory.

Climbing in was straightforward enough. Just inside the entrance the cavity opened to a high passageway, carved in chalk. It was extraordinary that I barely had to stoop as I made my way further into the darkness with the torch-beam lighting my way. The air was stale with the sweet stench of ancient death, growing stronger with every step, making me retch, but I continued on, further into the tunnel. I must be nearly there now, I told myself, to the point that the Midas had signalled above the ground hours earlier.

Though the risk that this area could also suffer subsidence was very real, I was beyond caring and simply too excited to give it a thought. Then the torch-beam ran over something bulky on the ground. I made to it and knelt down.

What lay before me, Clifford, was a very old

coarse knit sack, bulging at its sides. As I attempted to peel away the section that concealed its contents, the material simply disintegrated under touch and gold coins spilled out onto the ground around my knees. Hundreds of them, Clifford, absolutely hundreds, clinking into the silence around me. I picked one up and held it to the torchlight. It was heavy, old as the hills and smooth to the touch with an inscription across its surface that I could not make out in my inebriated state. I stuffed it into my pocket and laughed like a madman into the silence.

Then I saw them for the first time.

Beside the sack, slumped unevenly against the wall of the tunnel, was a robed figure. Whilst a hood covered his face, a skeletal hand was exposed at the cuff – yellowed skin stretched tightly over bone – the same as you might see in museums, in mummification sections. Next to him sat a smaller, crumpled shape, also robed and long dead. I recoiled as the torchlight illuminated his stretched, emaciated features and around the dark holes of his eye sockets.

I stumbled backwards, scrambling away from them, back towards the mouth of the tunnel and the safety of the cellar. But as I crawled through the opening and onto hard stone, I turned for a moment to look once more into the gaping darkness.

Just inside the edge of the tunnel came a quiet rustling, the sound of dry cloth brushing over stone. The atmosphere had changed now, malice a tangible force in the hissing silence.

A pale face emerged from the darkness and

though I barely glimpsed the sharp nose and glinting eyes against dried, taught skin, it was enough. I ran like a madman through the cellar and up into the house.

I slammed the living room door shut and sat shivering before the fire, hugging myself like a lunatic in an asylum, knowing what I *had* seen, but knowing also it was impossible. I thought of the shadow I had seen at the ruins, of the dark figure near the woodland and of my feelings of being watched, of never being completely alone here at Abbot's Keep. Was it possible that ghosts existed?

But then I turned to the facts, as we have always been taught, Clifford, and soon afterwards, my nerves calmed and I ran through it logically: I had drunk over half a bottle of whisky and then wine, some of which was nearly 20 years old. There had been an odd taste about the *Chateau Latour* which could account for the hallucination. Yes, there had been something in the wine, a toxin of some kind, that had created the illusion. I slouched back on the settee. Yes, that was all. Imaginings, nothing more.

I took the coin from my pocket and inspected it carefully under the lamp beside me – smooth, heavy, perfectly round in shape and most definitely gold. To be sure, I bit the edge gently until the surface yielded beneath the pressure, leaving a small dent where my tooth had been. The inscription across its face was clear now. Neat italics: *'Sequeris et onus feres'*

I had no idea what this meant but anyone with a 1st in Classics from Cambridge would, and

Alexander would be back in just a few hours.

In those quiet moments, with the rain beating at the blackened window beside me, the realisation of what I had found settled in. It changed everything. Yes, I would have to split the gold equally with Alexander but even then my share would be worth a fortune. Yes, Chip was dead but it had been an accident and I was vindicated now, through my discovery. I could buy a property, live comfortably, buy a new car, come to see you Clifford, and Annabelle, and spend time with little Harry, make amends, heal. Even Natalie would want me again now I finally had something to offer. So much to celebrate.

I jumped from my chair and screamed for joy. The noise echoed around the passageways of Abbot's Keep but soon afterwards the silence returned, more heavily than before, laced with tension.

But if this wasn't a cause for a celebration, then what was? I pushed the atlas away and grabbed the Colivettia from the alcove. I opened it and poured long, gulping measures down my throat. Ecstasy. I could buy another ten of these now if I chose to. But something was missing: Chip.

I rushed through to the outhouse and knelt beside the lifeless shape in the basket.

'Chip!' I unwrapped his body from the bloody towels. 'We found it, Chip. Well done, boy!'

I ran a hand across his cold, rigid body. Rigor mortis had firmly set in. Blank, sightless eyes. Lips curled and frozen in a ghastly wolf–like rictus, exposing sharp canines.

A chill crept over me. 'Alright, Chip. Sleep now.'

I staggered back to the living area, threw logs clumsily onto the fire and continued with the Colivettia.

Soon afterwards, I passed out. It was daylight when I woke, contorted and wretched, to the throaty roar of Alexander's Porsche on the driveway.

REVELATIONS

ABBOT'S KEEP

Still half-drunk, I staggered to my feet in panic as I heard bolts unlocking under key and the whining of the front door being opened.

A moment later, Alexander strode into the living room with arms outstretched.

'Foxey!' But the moment he saw me, he stopped in his tracks.

'You've fallen off, haven't you?' he said quietly, as though someone might hear. 'You stink like a bloody brewery, man.'

'I've been having kind of a . . . celebration.'

I watched his eyes move to the empty alcove where his treasured Colivettia had once sat, then shift to the fireplace where smashed glass lay scattered amongst the blackened ashes. I had no recollection of how it had come to be that way.

A noise in the corridor broke his concentration. I swayed unsteadily on my feet as I turned to see Natalie walk into the room.

She looked beautiful, Clifford. So extraordinarily beautiful. I had forgotten the effect her eyes had on me, so emerald and mystifying, making breath catch in my throat. For a moment I couldn't speak. My eyes scanned her slender neck, dark hair, full breasts, and then my heart sank. I could not believe it.

'You're pregnant.' I said it aloud, as though it might make sense if I actually heard the words. 'I mean . . .'

Alexander stepped forward. 'We wanted you to rest for a few days before we told you, Fox – '

'We?'

I turned to Natalie who was unable to meet my gaze now. She simply bowed her head.

'Look.' Alexander spread his fingers in the air as though about to play an invisible piano.

'A lot has changed since you went away, Foxey. People move on, you know, find another way. It's completel – '

'You two?' I laughed hysterically into the quietness. 'Together? And a child on the way?'

Suddenly, I understood it all.

Through my frenzied laughter, I realised there never had been a friend in Oxford. Natalie had told him that I was in rehabilitation in the Brentwell Unit. There never had been a wedding in Switzerland. They had been together all the time, probably close by. Perhaps even at my house in North Moreton. An amazing plan. I was to come out of rehabilitation and have a few days rest before they dropped the bombshell. And how it hit, Clifford. How it hit.

'That's brilliant!' I continued, laughing wildly. 'Just brilliant. Can I come to the wedding? No wait, I could be the best man. I mean – imagine the speech: *Natalie and my good old friend, Alexander, met whilst I was in rehab. Imagine my surprise when I came out months later to find that he'd been sleeping my wife, and had made her pregnant.*'

'I'm sorry, Foxey.'

'How long?'

'Since Henley last summer.' The response was swift and business-like, cutting straight through me. 'I am so sorr –'

'Save it, Alexander. You can't say anything now. Just save it. It is funny though.'

I put a hand in my pocket and found the coin, warm and smooth under my touch. I tossed it to Alexander.

He caught it with a confused look and inspected it carefully.

'That's right.' I pointed at him with a drunken finger. 'I found the gold. All of it. And there's a lot too. Much, much more than you ever thought. And you know what?' I pointed harder now. 'Half of it's fucking mine.'

'Where did you find it?' He was looking at the coin intently now. Natalie had joined him and was peering over his shoulder.

'Follow me.'

I headed for the cellar and as we descended the stony staircase Alexander asked, 'Where's Chip?'

'Oh, he's fine – just taking a rest in the outhouse. Hell of day we had yesterday . . . hell of a big fucking day.'

I smiled to myself a little then because suddenly I didn't feel quite so guilty anymore. He deserved it all, and more.

I pulled the drawstring in the main cellar, casting light over my work. Alexander gasped.

'Sweet Jesus. What have you done?' He scanned the piles of bricks; the hole in the eastern wall; the wine bottles lying across the floor.

'I think we should go back upstairs,' Natalie said calmly, as though I did not exist. 'He's drunk and this isn't right.'

'Fuck off then.' I spat the words out, feeling hatred boil to the surface. But then, just as quickly, I regained composure. 'I'm sorry. Seriously, it's all right. It's not a supporting wall. I'm an architect. I know these things.'

I picked up the torch, and a pointed spade, before ducking under the archway. Once inside, I sat the torch facing upwards in the middle of the floor, so that the room was illuminated in an orangey glow.

'This wall was built after the fire in 1912,' I said, leaning on the spade as they stepped through to join me. 'To the south here, is the mouth of the tunnel. It runs at least 120 metres, right through to the monastery ruins. Brilliant really. The gold's in there, less than five metres from where we stand – human remains too. Abbot Milroy and the boy, Goupil. Your history books were wrong, Alexander. They never were caught and tortured, and they never deserted the monastery with the gold either. They sealed themselves in the tunnel right here, taking fate into their own hands.'

Alexander stepped forward and peered into the gaping entrance of the tunnel. It was black as night in there.

'Jesus. How did you find it?'

'Chip found it,' I said. 'Incredible animal. He really *was* one hell of a dog. But you know that.'

I let the silence creep in, take over completely, as we stood in the gloom. I knew exactly what I had said, and the effect it would have.

'What do you mean, *was*?'

'Well he's dead, Alexander, just like the Abbot, just like Goupil, just like my marriage, just like you fucking are.'

With one massive swing I buried the spade deep into his face. It stuck for a moment, Clifford, and nothing happened. He just stared at me in the silence – strangely – as though confused by the fact that his face was literally split down the middle, but then the blood came and I knew, as I pulled it free, that he was finished. No one can survive a blow like that. Not that hard. Not that deep.

As he crumpled to the ground, Natalie tried to scream, but no sound came.

I think then, as she covered her mouth with her hands, that she was so frightened that her vocal chords had simply stopped working. But as I moved to her she did speak, her eyes wild with fear, like glistening stars in the torchlight.

'Simon, you can't.' She moved her hand to her swollen stomach, protecting the life within her. 'You cannot do that.'

I could only smile as I stepped forwards, forcing her back until she was flat against the eastern wall.

'It is a shame, Natalie. It really is, but it's for the best. For everyone.'

I drove the spade deep into her stomach and watched her eyes grow wide with terror. She coughed hard and spluttered blood over me as I drove the blade in again and again, until she quietened and slumped to the floor like a puppet without strings.

It was done, Clifford. There is nothing else.

But there was so much to do now, the task before me gigantic. As I wiped Natalie's blood from my face in the charged silence, nothing was insurmountable. I had changed once again. I was no longer the architect, Simon Fox, but so much more now: A murderer. I had crossed the line and anything was possible from this point forwards, the world at my feet once again, just as it had been all those years ago in Oxford, on graduation day. Only this time I would have it all. Every last coin.

I opened another bottle of *Chateau Latour* and set to work.

In the kitchen I found two frayed potato sacks, which I double–bagged to bear the weight of the gold. I took a shower too because my hands, face and neck were sticky with dried blood. It is messier than you think, Clifford, killing somebody with a spade.

Finally, standing at the top of the cellar steps, I took a swig of wine and grinned down into the blackness. It would soon be over. I would simply disappear and no one would ever know that I had been at Abbot's Keep. They would find the bodies eventually but it would be too late. I would be gone by then, far away.

Returning to the tunnel was harder than I had imagined. As I approached the yawning entrance I struggled to push away thoughts of the face I had seen before, wrinkled and cadaverous, but knew there was no option. I climbed inside, with sacks and torch in hand.

The muffled pattering of rain sounded above me as I made my way further into the chalky darkness, my torch beam shining out before me like a beacon, picking out the roughly carved walls.

I strode forwards with feigned courage until the decaying nest of old sacking came into view. Painfully aware of my noise roaring in the quietness, I knelt and began transferring the coins into the new sack, refraining from looking up, further along the tunnel, where I had seen the remains of Abbot Milroy and the boy. As I continued, the silence grew thick, brimming with tension and anger. The foul stench of rotten flesh filled the air around me until my breaths became laboured. Finally, I lifted the sack over my shoulder and retched like a sick animal as I staggered back to the tunnel's entrance.

It was heavy, Clifford, so very heavy, to pull the sack through that hole and onto solid ground.

Once there, I made to the main cellar area. But as I did a cold hand gripped at my ankle. I screamed and kicked free, lurching for the archway that would take me to the safety beyond. But I stopped short, because I suddenly realised whose hand it was.

I turned and shone the torch towards the floor where Natalie lay, not quite dead yet, but curled foetus-like, slowly writhing in a great pool of thickening blood. I left the sack just inside the archway and returned to her, crouching whilst I shone the torch in her face.

Near death, her breaths were shallow and barely audible. Blood dripped from her mouth as she whispered.

'Please...Simon...don't leave me here...'

'Don't worry,' I touched her face tenderly. 'You'll be happy here together. It's what you wanted.'

'. . . Don't leave me here. . .with them.'

Then I heard it in the darkness, in the farthest recess of the gloom. A quiet sweeping noise, cloth passing over stone. Then, just on the edge of hearing, a slight clicking, like the sound of a wet mouth opening and closing.

I beamed the torch about the room. Nothing, only the charred brickwork, the solitary cast-iron crucifix hanging on the wall.

I turned back to Natalie and watched the final breath leave her in an agonizing groan. She stared straight at me, as though deeply concerned for my welfare, but I knew she was gone.

I lifted her from the floor and pushed her motionless body through the entrance to the tunnel until I heard it land with a thump on the other side.

Next was Alexander. He was heavier of course and it took every ounce of strength to elevate his body to the dark hole and cram his lifeless, bloody form inside. Before I let go, I stared into his broken face, at the deep gash running through his cheek and nose.

'Thanks for having me, old boy.' I whispered.

The rest was easy. I returned the bookshelf to its original position, concealing once again the entrance to the tunnel. Next, in the main cellar area, I removed the wine bottles from their neat little beds and unscrewed the wooden rack from its fittings.

Once I had re-fastened it to cover the archway on the eastern wall and replaced the bottles, everything looked perfect. I piled the loose bricks in the farthest corner of the cellar and then dragged the sack up the cellar steps and locked the door behind me. Done.

I washed my hands in the white-enamel kitchen sink and watched, mesmerised, as blood spiralled into the drain and out of sight, just like my hopes of a future with Natalie.

I was trembling like an old dog so I opened a new bottle of whisky and drank until my throat hurt and my nerves settled. It seemed easier after that, to drag the sack upstairs to my bedroom where I sat and drank more, watching light fade across the fields and clouds gather into a deep, apocalyptic redness overhead. I was drunk and the hours had somehow slipped away from me.

How could it possibly be evening so soon?

I let the heavy coins slip between my fingers and back into the sack, wondering where I should go, how I could spend the money, what future I could carve out for myself.

Tomorrow, I decided, after a long rest, I would leave Abbot's Keep forever and begin my life all over again.

I woke suddenly in the night to a loud crashing noise from somewhere downstairs.

I thought of the bookcase in the cellar, the one that covered the tunnel, and wondered what kind of noise it would make if it fell to the floor; if it were pushed over from the inside. But it was impossible of course.

Then another noise; a clinking of some kind, like the sound of wine bottles rolling across smooth stone, then a slow creaking noise; a door whining open downstairs? But I was too drunk to move and so I closed my eyes again.

Later, I came around to the terrible realisation I was no longer alone in the bedroom.

Moonlight shone in long silvery beams across the room, illuminating all but the darkest recesses. A whispering sound nearby sent a chill through me, right to the bone, but when I tried to turn my head found that I could not.

But I could see now, from the corner of my eye, a stooped figure – hooded, robed in a monk's habit and very tall – standing away from me, near the doorway. Then a smaller figure, also robed, came into view. Their raspy breaths broke the silence and then the boy turned and began to push a small cart in my direction, its wooden wheels squeaking and rattling across the floorboards toward my bed, closer and closer still.

For a moment the moonlight shone across his dried face. I tried to scream, but the only sound that came was a low moaning, as though I had been anaesthetised and rendered unable to move a single muscle, even in my throat. I could only watch as the boy hobbled toward me, pushing the cart before him.

I could see more clearly now. Not a cart, but a wooden table of some kind, set on wheels, with black metal implements lying neatly across its surface. What were they? I could barely make them out in the gloom: A long iron rod with a sharp hook at one end, a pair of scissor type tools, with elongated handles – like something a blacksmith might use. But not a blacksmith, Clifford, that isn't quite right, and it wasn't a pair of scissors either. It was a hoof parer. A farrier's hoof parer.

I moaned again as the Abbot turned. His habit brushed against the floor and as he leant over me his yellowed skin tightened to a leering grin.

His eyes – so very black – disappeared into darkness. I struggled to turn away, to reel from the stench of death, but could not move. He leant closer and his dry tongue slithered about his dead mouth.

'Sequeris et onus feres,' he whispered.

Then it began, as I knew it would; the tongue first, easily pierced with the iron hook and prised from my mouth, stretched tight for the hoof parer's blades.

I moaned pathetically as pain reeked through me. They moved methodically, clanking the bloodied tools in the moonlight and rasping out breaths around my face. Next, the ears, and I focussed my mind in an attempt to escape the pain. If I could just become angry then it would go away. If I could just summon the rage and divert my attention completely then it would be over.

And so I thought of you Clifford, thought of the Stanford building, thought of how you had turned me away when I had asked for your help, when I had sought your council to defend the numerous lawsuits against me. A *Conflict of Interest*. That is what you had called it.

Yes, that had been your feeble excuse. There are not many barristers who specialise in construction disputes, Clifford, and you are undoubtedly the best. But even though we were flesh and blood, you turned me away. We both know why. It was not a *Conflict of Interest*, Clifford, but a knowledge that you may lose the case and that would never have done, would it? With the infamous Stanford failure printed indelibly onto your Curriculum Vitae you would never have achieved the Queen's Council. Not in a million years. And that was more important than anything, wasn't it? More important than me, more important than my falling to bankruptcy. More important than blood itself.

I groaned as withered fingers peeled away my bed covers, because I knew it was not over. Do you know what it means to be gelded, Clifford?

Tonight, the sea stretches out before me as I rest on the pebbles. Moonlight glimmers across its dark surface like thousands of wriggling fish and, as waves lap and suck at the shoreline, gulls wing above me; their sharp calls like taunting laughs in the night.

Milroy and the boy have led me around the coastline for some weeks now, searching for the right place, but it never ends. You will ask why I do not just turn, just run, and keep running, but they always come back, Clifford, and I still have much to lose.

After all, I still have my sight, and my sense

of smell but things can always change. It is a heavy burden, but I will continue.

No, do not try to follow me, Clifford. No good can come of it. I bid you farewell, my brother. Rest easy – for even though I have never heard the word that I most wanted to hear from you, I forgive it all.

God bless you and your family.

Simon

ABBOT'S KEEP

REUNIONS

ABBOT'S KEEP

Bentley Head
Near Dover

12th December 1980

Annabelle

You were right all along. I should never have come to
this forsaken place. A week has passed and you will
be worried sick, terrified even, for my safety. I am so
sorry, my dearest Annabelle, but it is too late now.

After all I had seen at Abbot's Keep, I did not
return to The Weary Friar but instead followed the
trail – to find Simon – and in doing so led myself into
the waiting darkness. I found him, far from anywhere,
at Bentley Head, south of Dover. I will send this to
you when I have a chance, although it may not be for
some time. There are other considerations for me
now. Unspeakable considerations.

I tried to telephone after I had been to the
house, as promised, but the lines must still have been
down in Oswaldkirk. All I got was the blank tone. In
any case, you would have tried again to dissuade me
and my mind was made up – even more so once I had
visited Abbot's Keep.

I should have known I suppose, the moment I
saw Everett–Heath's Porsche in the driveway, beside

Simon's old Volvo, that there was truth in it, but I had to be sure.

After trying the outer doors several times I took a crowbar from the boot of the Jaguar and wrenched the lock on the front door until it gave.

Inside, the house was like a tomb. That is the only way that I can describe it. There was a stillness about the place, as though no life was here, or ever had been, but at the same time the house seemed to watch silently as I moved from room to room, putting into place all that Simon had outlined in his account.

In the living area: broken glass scattered about the hearth, an empty alcove where the Colivettia had once sat. In the outhouse: flies buzzing crazily around the wretched body of a dead Springer Spaniel. In the bedroom upstairs: blood-covered sheets, an ancient looking trolley on wooden wheels beside the bed. And then, of course, the cellar: smashed wine bottles strewn about the floor, the heavy stench of alcohol and death permeating the air, a fallen wine rack, exposing the rough archway in the eastern wall. Then beyond that, into the darkness, the heady odour becoming stronger as I stepped over the fallen bookcase and towards the tunnel's entrance.

Oh, Annabelle, the horror as my torch beam found their lifeless corpses sprawled across the chalky ground.

I had never seen a dead body in the flesh before, but knew immediately that something was wrong. It was as though they had laid there not for just weeks, but years; as though every last nutrient had been sucked from them, leaving behind only the dried, emaciated shells that had once housed their souls.

For a moment, the torch illuminated Natalie's shrivelled features and the ghastly look stretched across her face. I ran then, ran from Abbot's Keep, to the Jaguar where I sat for many minutes regaining composure and bringing logic to the forefront.

I began to piece it together: Simon, already drunk from the Colivettia, had exploded with rage at the news of Natalie's relationship with Alexander. After murdering them, he had hidden their bodies in the cellar and continued drinking throughout the day and into the evening.

He had become unhinged and then, as guilt overcame him, had mutilated his own body. Later, he had staggered into the countryside and, haunted by his actions, had created a dark, imaginary world, borne of remorse and a futile desire to escape all that he had left behind at Abbot's Keep; a world in which Abbot Milroy and the boy, Antonio Goupil, forced him to continue walking.

I knew then, sitting in the Jaguar beneath the ancient structure of the house, that before I disclosed information to the Police, I would try and find Simon and force him to give himself up. Courts are more lenient on murderers who step forward and show regret. It is the least I could do, Annabelle, having let him down so badly in the past.

How wrong I was, once again, to make that final, irreversible decision.

There are only two disused lighthouses on the eastern coast and so I took a chance that it was Sittinghead Rock, just short of Hythe. I was right. The lock had been broken and just inside the doorway a large chunk of driftwood laid across the metal floor. At the top of the winding staircase, the rounded observatory was just as Simon had described: the crab shells, the rotting seagull – no more than mess of feather and bone.

Then something glimmered, just beside the yellowed skull of the bird. A single, shining coin.

Against what I perceived to be an irrational urge to recoil, I crouched and lifted it from the ground. It was heavy and definitely gold. The inscription was perfectly clear: *Sequeris et onus feres*

I slipped it into my pocket and stood.

From this vantage point, high above the sea, I could make out a pebble beach further down the coast.

I got back into the Jaguar and, once nearby,

stood on the cliff face to gaze down at the cove. There was no sign of him and so I followed the coastal road, nearer and nearer to Dover, always with one eye scanning the landscape for a solitary figure on the hillsides, for any movement on the beaches below.

As I approached the grassy picnic area on the cliffs at Bentley Head, I saw movement on the sands, a dark figure with a rucksack over his back, trudging wearily in amongst the ragged line of seaweed near the break of the shoreline. I stopped the car and made for the cliff edge, staring as I did the hundreds of feet below into the narrow horseshoe cove. It was him, Annabelle. It was Simon. I would know my own brother anywhere, even at this distance.

'Simon!' I shouted against the wind.

He turned then, lifting his face to the cliff where I stood.

'Simon!' I waved my arms. He saw me.

From here, he was no more than a small dark figure with a pallid face. But I could see his mouth moving, just as in my dreams, and no sound came. It was lost in the wind. His pale face wore the same forlorn expression, the one that I had never wished to see.

As I stared down to the cove, I saw that Simon had begun moving again, more arduously now, under the weight of the rucksack. I saw also he was not alone on the beach, but that there were two other figures, pulling a small wooden rowing–boat across the sand, towards the water.

Simon was a long way from them, but moving steadily in their direction all the time.

They looked like monks, dressed in black habits as they were, and one was far taller than the other. But it was coincidence, I told myself, pure and simple, and made my way down to Simon.

Minutes later, with sea spray skimming off the water and stinging at my face, I stepped onto the beach and ran against the wind to him. But he staggered away from me, as though in terrible fear, limping and lurching like a maimed animal towards the monks at the end of the shoreline.

I stopped him with a forceful tug on his rucksack and he buckled under the weight, falling to his knees.

He peered up and moaned into the wind, and his face, encrusted with blood and sand and dirt, sent my blood cold, because in his pleading, glaring eyes I saw the horror more clearly than words could ever have described, even if he had been able to speak.

He lifted a piece of gnarled driftwood from the dried seaweed beside him and scratched letters into the sand: *Go Now. Go.*

It is worthy of ridicule but – despite everything, in that moment – I was taken to another time, a time when we were children, brothers, playing without care or fear, writing messages in the sand to one another and laughing into the sunshine.

The moment did not last long, Annabelle, for when I looked up to see the monks steadily approaching, I realised that everything Simon had written had been the truth, and also that it was too late for me to simply go. I was wrong about everything.

I must finish this now, before they return. The silence is here again. They always come in the silence. Just as Simon said, they are never far away.

I could tell more, of the horrors, but where is the need? What good would it do? At least we are together, I suppose. Brothers, once again.

I would telephone you, but there is little point. We are the same now, you see, Simon and I.

I will write again soon but do not try to follow us. This is the darkest place you could imagine. I would not wish it upon any soul, living or dead.

I love you, and Harry, more than life itself and I am so sorry for everything. I will try to get back but it is difficult. They always come, you see. I must go.

Clifford

Creswell Manor
Oswaldkirk
Yorkshire

8th March 1981

Clifford

I write this letter knowing that it will never leave
Creswell Manor. After a time, the loneliness becomes
unbearable and sometimes I find myself writing these
letters to you, knowing that you will never see their
content. But it matters little. It is just words on a
page. Nothing more. No harm can come of it. The
harm is already done.

Hopes of finding you fade further with each
sunset that falls across Oswaldkirk valley. In my
heart, I know you will never return to Yorkshire.
Your path is set in stone.

Harry is growing fast. He talks about you
every day, but it is strange. After three months, it is
as though he has come to accept that he will not see
you now. Children are so adaptable, aren't they? Why
cannot it not be the same for me?

The papers loved it of course: dead bodies
hidden in the cellar of an ancient house; a missing
architect and barrister. A Jaguar abandoned on the
cliff top at Bentley Head. The Fabulous Fox brothers,
Oxford graduates from the wealthiest stock, hunted
for murder. But soon it was over because you were
nowhere. Even the Police do not understand how you

could have disappeared without trace. But I know.

'Sequeris et onus feres'

It means, 'You shall follow and carry the burden.'

That is where you are now. I see you in my nightmares, Clifford, your pale mouth stretching in the darkness, unable to speak because your tongue is cut out. Yes, you and Simon are the same now. You simply follow, and carry the burden.

It came to me last night, as I lay alone in our bed – the small detail that had niggled me on reading Simon's account for the first time. The detail that had bothered and eluded us both.

It was Paris, Clifford. You remember. L'Eglise de St Mathieu. After we had listened to the nuns sing, we went to the crypt.

You were looking for verification of your ancestry, searching for your name on the tomb stones set into the walls, or rather the French translation of 'Fox', which is Renard.

The name did not appear on any of the stones, not one. You asked one of the nuns in your stuttering French and she led us to a dark corner of the crypt, where candles barely lit the walls. She pointed to a stone that read, Goupil. You shook your head but thanked her anyway, and we left.

But she was right, Clifford. Renard is a modern word, only used in recent times because mentioning the word 'fox' was considered bad luck amongst farmers. The old French word for 'fox', is 'goupil.'

Today, I did a little digging of my own.

The church itself, L'Eglise de St Mathieu, is so called because it houses bones believed to have belonged to St Mathew. The church acquired the relics in 1531 when a passing monk, Abbot Milroy, and his aid, Antonio Goupil, sold the relics to the nuns in exchange for gold.

Over a hundred years earlier, in 1412, the nuns were sold a collection of other relics by a tall monk, travelling with a young boy by the name of Volpe. It is Italian, Clifford. It means 'fox'.

That's the trouble with the past. It never goes away. It just waits and waits until someone digs it up again. I pray at least that you have made peace with Simon over the Stanford business. At least you are together, as you say, but Simon was right, you know. You are not *estranged*. You are lost.

Remember you used to say that it is all superstition, that everything can be explained away. How wrong you must realise you were now Clifford, as you follow with the burden.

I will be sure not to let Harry seek his roots.

I love you. Forever.

Annabelle

CONCLUSION

ABBOT'S KEEP

Fox & Burrows
Lendin Cellars
York

13 March 1981

Dear Annabelle

I trust you are as well as can be expected under the circumstances.

Three months is a very long time to worry over the safety of a loved one and our thoughts here at the Firm go out to you, and to Harry. We will, of course, continue to pay Clifford's salary into your account indefinitely, so please have no concern in this respect. He is, as you know, a dear friend to us all here. We will continue to support you financially and emotionally. You only need ask, and we will deliver.

I believe it only appropriate to write at this time to inform you of the Partner's intentions in this matter. Firstly, I will say that we are unanimous in our view that Thames Valley Police have been nothing short of useless in their endeavours to locate Clifford. My own research into their progress has highlighted that their investigation lacks both significant information and resource, but above all is deficient of motivation and the momentum that is, in my experience, critical in the delivery of results. There is no doubt in our collective mind that the police investigation will remain fruitless for the foreseeable future. For these reasons, we have decided to take matters into our own hands and will be using our own, more reliable methods to locate Clifford and bring him back to you.

In the legal world, private agencies are frequently employed to unearth information that would not normally be obtainable through the usual channels. We are approaching this matter in the same way and have taken it upon ourselves to utilise an asset that we know to be effective. His name is Jakob Fuchs and he is without doubt the most relentless private investigator we have ever come across. He will simply not stop until he finds the truth, wherever it may lie.

We call him our Little Fox, not only because he is a man of small stature and is able to burrow deeply beneath the surface, but because the German translation of his name has the same meaning.

I will of course keep you updated with our progress and be in touch shortly.

Keep strong and fear not. We will find Clifford, whatever the cost.

Yours sincerely

Wilfred Burrows QC

THE END

ABBOT'S KEEP

By the Same Author

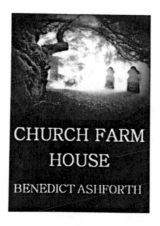

Spanning four decades, the dark history of Church Farm House is explored within four interlinking horror stories. Welcome to the nightmare . . .

Available now on Amazon Kindle

Coming Soon . . .

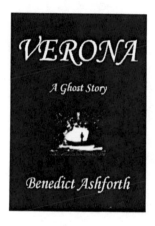

An infertile couple escape to Italy for a short break but soon realise they are not alone, and that a long-forgotten evil has awoken.

Scheduled for release winter 2014

ABBOT'S KEEP

About the Author

Benedict Ashforth lives in Dorset, England, with wife,
Lynne, and son, Antony.
Benedict was born in Redhill, Surrey, and was
schooled at Ampleforth College in North Yorkshire.

Follow Benedict on Twitter or email him:

https://twitter.com/HorrorFly
benedict2012@hotmail.co.uk

ABBOT'S KEEP

Did You Enjoy ABBOT'S KEEP?

Your feedback is immensely important
to the author.

For all of your comments – positive
or negative – please post your review
on Amazon.